"I'm scared, Liam. I don't know what's going on, or what I'm supposed to do."

"Don't worry, Gabby," Liam said over the phone. "We'll make sure you and Mia are safe."

Gabby glanced in the rearview mirror, thankful that Mia was finally sleeping. There was a black pickup behind her. Was that the same one she'd noticed earlier?

"Gabby? Are you...there?"

The call was breaking up.

Gabby gave the car all the gas she could and flew back up the hill. All she had to do was get to the nearby sleepy tourist town and she would be fine.

She glanced again in the rearview mirror. The black pickup was still there.

"Liam..."

"What's...on...Gabby..."

The car behind her smashed into her bumper. Mia woke up and started crying. Gabby fought to keep the car on the road...

Lisa Harris is a Christy Award winner and winner of the Best Inspirational Suspense Novel for 2011 from *RT Book Reviews*. She and her family are missionaries in southern Africa. When she's not working, she loves hanging out with her family, cooking different ethnic dishes, photography and heading into the African bush on safari. For more information about her books and life in Africa, visit her website at lisaharriswrites.com.

Books by Lisa Harris

Love Inspired Suspense

Final Deposit
Stolen Identity
Deadly Safari
Taken
Desperate Escape
Desert Secrets
Fatal Cover-Up
Deadly Exchange
No Place to Hide
Sheltered by the Soldier

Visit the Author Profile page at Harlequin.com.

SHELTERED BY THE SOLDIER

LISA HARRIS

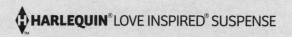
HARLEQUIN® LOVE INSPIRED® SUSPENSE

Recycling programs
for this product may
not exist in your area.

LOVE INSPIRED BOOKS

ISBN-13: 978-1-335-67896-6

Sheltered by the Soldier

Copyright © 2019 by Lisa Harris

www.Harlequin.com

Printed in U.S.A.

I will lift up mine eyes unto the hills, from whence cometh my help. My help cometh from the Lord, which made heaven and earth. He will not suffer thy foot to be moved: he that keepeth thee will not slumber.
—Psalms 121:1-3

To those longing for strength when hard times hit.
May you find your protection in Him.

ONE

Gabriella Kensington balanced her eleven-month-old daughter Mia on her hip while fighting to get the key into the sticky lock of the back door of her townhouse. The next time she went out, she was going to have to buy a can of WD-40 and fix it. She considered setting the two plastic grocery bags hanging from her wrist down on the porch, but the three inches of snow that had blanketed the city last night from a late fall cold front had left the mostly uncovered surface both slippery and wet.

But she'd worry about that another day.

She wiggled the handle, heard the click, then finally opened the door. Heat from the house rushed out and filled her lungs with warmth.

Gabby stepped inside as an unexpected chill sliced through her. Setting the two plastic bags of groceries onto the counter, she glanced around the kitchen, managing to knock one of the bags over in the process. A grapefruit rolled off the counter and onto the floor, but she hardly noticed.

Instead, she stared into the living room that opened up from the kitchen. The entire room had been trashed. Papers had been dumped from her desk. Drawers pulled open and their contents dumped. Books and photos lay scattered across the hardwood floor. Mia started fussing. Gabby had no idea if whoever had done this was still somewhere in the house, but there was no time to find out.

This can't be happening.

But the frightening text she'd received two days ago, demanding her to stop asking questions and threatening her and her daughter, only served to confirm her worst fears. Adrenaline pumping, she hushed her daughter who was struggling to get down. She couldn't take any chances in case someone was still in the house. Not with Mia. Instead, she raced back to the car, fumbled with the straps on the car seat while Mia's fussing grew louder.

"It's okay, sweet baby. Nothing's going to happen to you. Mama's going to make sure of that."

A lump swelled in her throat as she slid into the car. She wanted to pray, except she knew God didn't always answer prayers. If someone was after her, she was on her own.

Hands shaking, she turned the key in the ignition. The car refused to start.

No...no...no...

"Not now. Please...not now."

She glanced back at the house, terrified that at any moment someone was going to burst out of the back door and come after her. If someone had still been in the house, she had no doubt that they'd heard Mia crying. She turned the key again to start the engine. Her father had tried to convince her to replace her jeep with something more reliable, but it was going to take her another year to save up. Now she couldn't help but wonder if she should have tried to make it work.

A third try and the engine caught.

Letting out a strong huff of relief, she pulled out of the driveway, her heart still racing. Calling 911 was the logical option, but something made her hesitate. The letters her husband had written her before his death while still deployed had left her shaken. And this happening so soon after she'd questioned his commanding officers made her wonder if she'd managed to ask the wrong person, triggering something she was at a loss of how to handle. Which meant if someone was after her, she had no idea how far their arm might reach. She stopped at a red light, then glanced at the leather bag with Will's letters on the floor-board of the car. That had to be what they were after. She swallowed hard. No. She was sounding paranoid. But Will had been paranoid, too. So maybe her fear stemming from the last letter he'd written her wasn't that far off after all.

I think they realize I've been looking into the paper trail. I need to go to some-one with what I have, but I have to make sure the evidence is solid. Some of these contractors are the kind of people who wouldn't hesitate at defrauding our gov-ernment. The kind of people who wouldn't blink at killing anyone who got in their way.

The light turned green and she headed north toward the freeway. She'd memorized the de-tails of Will's letters. They had mentioned con-tracted workers, so she'd assumed that going to someone in the military was safe. But clearly, she'd been mistaken. And now she couldn't af-ford to trust the wrong person again. It wasn't worth risking her daughter's life. But either way, she needed a plan and the best option seemed to be to get as far away from here as she could.

But where? The digital clock on the dash said it was a quarter to three. She could call her parents, but what could they do? They were currently enjoying Florida's balmy weather and couldn't exactly help her. She had friends that would take her in, but there was no way she was going to put someone else's life at risk. And until she figured out who was behind this, she'd never be safe. Will was dead, and she had Mia to protect.

Her mind shifted gears as she upped her speed and merged onto the freeway. There was one person who might be able to help her. She glanced at the phone laying in the console next to her. One person who might have the answers to whoever was behind this.

Liam O'Callaghan.

She tried to push the name out of her mind, and instead glanced at the line of cars behind her as each mile took her farther way from danger—and closer to the town of Timber Falls near where he lived. She hadn't heard from Liam for several weeks. He and Will had been deployed together, then Liam had spent months in both inpatient and outpatient rehabilitation with injuries from the blast that killed her husband. Over the past year and a half, he'd called at least once a month to check on her and make sure she was doing okay and had even come to see her several times. But she hadn't missed the hint of guilt in his voice each time. As if what had happened to Will was somehow his fault. And she was clearly a reminder.

She placed the call on the cheap smart phone she'd picked up yesterday before she had a chance to change her mind again. But instead of him answering, it switched to voice mail.

"Liam, this is Gabby." She paused, wondering if she was doing the right thing. Wondering why she felt so hesitant in asking for his help. She tried to shake off the tension in her voice. "Listen… I need to talk to you. It's important. Please. Call me back as soon as you can on this number."

Gabby hung up the call, then glanced into the rearview mirror at the back seat where Mia sat in her car seat, playing with her stuffed giraffe. At least she'd stopped crying. When Gabby had found out she was pregnant, everything had seemed so perfect. She'd had the perfect marriage, perfect family, perfect life. Then in one life-altering moment, two uniformed officers had shown up at her front door and everything changed.

Her phone rang, pulling her back into the

present. She pushed the call-answer button on the steering wheel. "Liam?"

"Gabby...are you okay?"

"Not really." She didn't want to tell him what was going on—that would only make the situation more real—but neither could she put the life of her daughter at risk. "I need help, and I didn't know who else to call."

She glanced back into the rearview mirror. Mia had thrown down the giraffe and was fussing again, but Gabby couldn't stop the car. Couldn't take any risks that might jeopardize her baby's life more than she already had.

"What happened?" he asked.

She swallowed hard, trying to dismiss the feeling she was being followed. "I got home this afternoon and discovered someone had ransacked my place."

"Wait a minute... Have you called 911?"

"I was scared and panicked. Afraid someone might still be in the house."

"I understand, but you need to call the authorities."

She hesitated. "I can't."

"Why not?"

The last thing she wanted to do was get Liam involved, but what other option did she have?

"Gabby...what's going on?"

"There's something I need to talk to you about. There have been other threats—"

"Threats? Is that why you have a new number?"

"I was afraid someone might have been tracking my phone, but I'd rather discuss everything in person."

"Where are you now?" he asked.

She glanced at the clock. "I'm about twenty minutes from Timber Falls. If you could meet me in town—"

"Of course. Or you could come out to the ranch."

"I don't want to get your family involved."

"Will was my best friend. I promised him if anything ever happened to him, I'd make sure you and Mia were okay. I owe him my life. My family understands that."

She looked around, her chest still heaving. Sirens wailed from a wreck on the other side of the highway.

"Is there a chance anyone is following you?" he asked.

"I don't think so, but I can't be sure. Traffic's pretty heavy, and it's starting to snow."

"I'm out at the ranch, but I'll head to town now. It will take me at least thirty minutes, but you can wait for me at the sheriff's office on the edge of town. It's well lit. You can't miss it."

"Okay."

"Do you remember meeting my brother Griffin?"

"Yes."

She'd met his entire family at Will's funeral, and while most of that day was a blur, she remembered being impressed with the four brothers and their parents, whose ancestors had first settled in this area three generations ago.

"I'll call him. Griffin's a deputy and on duty today. I'll give him a heads-up."

She drew in a long, slow breath, trying to gather her nerves. "I'm scared, Liam. I don't know what's going on, or what I'm supposed to do."

"Don't worry. We're going to find a way to make sure you and Mia are safe until we figure out what's going on."

She glanced in the rearview mirror, thankful that Mia was finally sleeping. Poor baby was missing her nap and was exhausted. Her gaze shifted slightly as something else caught her attention. There was a black pickup behind her, following too close. Had she seen the same vehicle earlier?

Her fingers gripped the steering wheel. Five seconds later, the road straightened and headed down another narrow mountainous stretch. She pressed harder on the accelerator as she sucked in a deep breath and tried to talk herself down. No one had followed her out of her neighborhood. This was nothing more than her imagination playing tricks on her.

She gave the car all the gas she could and flew back up the hill. A stab of pain shot through her head, and she realized she'd been clenching her jaw. The stress from the last few days had managed to consume her. She kept her eyes on the road, her hand steady on the wheel as she passed a sign to Timber Falls. All she had to do was get to the sleepy tourist town and she would be fine.

"Gabby? Are you…there?"

The call was breaking up.

She glanced again in the rearview mirror. The black pickup was still there. "Liam…"

"What's…on… Gabby…"

The car behind her smashed into her bumper. She fought to keep the car on the road as she pushed on the pedal. Mia woke up and started crying.

For the first time in months, Gabby prayed God would intervene.

Liam pressed on the gas pedal, pushing the speed limit down the narrow two-lane road that led from the O'Callaghan Ranch toward Timber Falls, the nearest town from his family's ten-thousand-plus acre ranch. He called Gabby back.

Nothing.

He tried to ignore the list of uncertainties simmering beneath the surface. He needed to stop worrying. Phone service around the ranch and the road leading into Timber Falls had always left holes of no reception in spite of recent upgrades over the past couple years. It didn't mean something had happened. This had been his life the past few months. Waiting for the ball to drop, dumping another tragedy on him. His mother kept reminding him that he wasn't living. And yet, he knew he hadn't really been living for a long time.

Not since Will had died and Liam had been life-flighted to Germany, almost losing his own life alongside his best friend.

He tried to shake off the memories and instead focus on the road. The last thing he needed to do was run into a deer on the long stretch of winding road toward town. Gabby was fine. One of them had just gone through a no-service patch. He'd meet up with her, see what she needed, then go on with his own life.

Because if he were honest with himself, seeing Gabby was the last thing he wanted to do.

Months of therapy had finally gotten him to the place he needed to be physically, but emotionally the scars were yet to completely heal. And seeing Gabby again… He knew it was only going to be a reminder of what happened that night to his best friend. But he couldn't let emotion rule his thoughts. He owed Will his life on more than one occasion and if that meant ensuring Gabby and her baby were safe, then he planned on doing anything in his power to keep them that way.

Memories from the night of Will's death refused to leave him alone, bringing back the all-too-familiar panic. They'd been ambushed that starless night only a few miles from the base while out on a routine patrol in Afghanistan. But there was nothing routine about what had happened that night. By the time he got to Will, his friend was already dead.

Mercifully, his memories of that night were few and far between. The following minutes and hours had dragged by as comrades fought to get him to safety. Over a year later, there were still moments when he wished he'd died instead of his friend. Will had a wife and daughter. He should have lived. And yet, for some reason God had taken Will and let Liam live. The guilt of that loss had yet to let go of him completely. But if he could help

Will's widow, it seemed the least he could do to make amends.

He tried to call her again, but for a third time, the call wouldn't go through. This time he called a different number.

"Griffin?"

"Hey," his older brother said. "I was just planning on calling you. Are we still on for tomorrow night—"

"Yeah, but listen. I've got a problem, and I'm going to need your help. Do you remember Gabby Kensington?"

"Of course. Will's wife."

"Yes. She's on her way into town now to see me. I'm not sure exactly what's going on, but apparently her house was burglarized. She's scared, and our call got disconnected."

"You know how sketchy phone service is in the passes leading up here. I'm sure she's fine."

"I know, but I'm still worried. I'm on my way into town now, but you're closer than I am."

"What kind of vehicle is she driving?"

"She owns a yellow jeep."

"Don't worry. I'll head south out of town right now and see if I can find her. Keep me updated on your location and we'll meet up. In the meantime, try to keep calling her, but send me her number so I can try as well."

Twenty minutes later, Timber Falls began to show above the horizon. He'd grown up in this town. Graduated from the local high school. And for the past few weeks, it had been the place where he could work on the family ranch alongside his older brother, Caden, while he continued to heal. He wanted to go back to active duty, but the doctors still hadn't approved him. Which left his future in the military hanging in the balance.

Liam's phone rang, jerking him from his thoughts. "Griffin?"

"I found her."

"Where is she?"

"First of all, she and her daughter are both fine," Griffin said, answering Liam's next question before he had a chance to ask it. "We're heading back into town now."

"What's going on?"

"You did the right thing to call me, because there are a couple things you need to know before you see her."

Liam felt a shot of adrenaline rush through him. "What do you mean?"

"I haven't had time to take an official statement yet, but someone rammed into her from behind while she was on her way here." Griffin hesitated. "From the way she described it, this wasn't an accident."

"But she's okay?"

"She's fine. Just meet me at the sheriff's office."

Five minutes later, Liam parked in front of the square brick building on the edge of town, then hurried inside.

"Liam…" Angie Baker, the department's secretary, looked up from her computer as he stepped into the lobby. "I just got off the phone with Deputy O'Callaghan. He's almost here."

"Thank you."

He started pacing the white tiled floor while Angie went back to her computer. The clock on the wall ticked by the seconds. But he couldn't find a way to shove aside the guilt. If anything happened to Gabby, he'd never forgive himself.

"You're going to wear a hole in the floor." Angie stood up and grabbed a file from a tray. "Can I get you some coffee?"

"No. I'm fine." He stopped pacing and forced a smile at the offer. "But thanks."

Ten minutes later, Griffin finally walked into the lobby from the back. The two of them might be brothers, but while Griffin had brown hair, brown eyes and a knack for management, Liam had blond hair, blue eyes and an affinity for strategizing and problem solving. Though their looks and even personalities might be different, there was one thing they had in common. They both had a strong sense of duty and justice neither could ignore.

"Griffin…" He didn't even try to curb his impatience as he crossed the room. "Where are they?"

"I took them directly through the back door to the conference rooms. Thought she might be more comfortable there. I also asked Mom to come over from the clinic, so she could check them out."

"But Gabby's really alright?"

"She's shook up, but yes. Apparently, the car that hit her spun out in the snow, and she managed to lose them."

"Do you have any idea who hit her?"

"I've got a deputy looking into the incident, but the chances of us finding them are slim in this weather. What about you? She didn't say much except that she'd been threatened before. Did she give you any clue as to who might be after her?"

"No. That's why I need to talk with her." Liam weighed his options, then made a decision. "I'm going to take her out to the ranch until we can figure out what's going on. A burglary is one thing, but almost getting run off the road means all of this isn't random. And from what I can tell, she doesn't think so, either. I've known Gabby for several years and she's not the kind of woman to borrow trouble. Something is very wrong."

"I agree." Griffin pulled off his deputy hat and scratched the back of his head. "You can come back with me now. Then as soon as she's given her statement and Mom has cleared them medically, you can take them out to the ranch. If we need her for anything else, I'll know where she is."

And he'd be able to ensure she stayed safe.

A minute later, Liam walked into the small conference room where Gabby was standing near the window. He crossed the room, then pulled her into his arms and hugged her. "Gabby... I'm so, so sorry."

"I'm fine, really. Just shook up."

She looked at him with those big brown eyes of hers. He'd gone to visit her half a dozen times since Will's death seventeen months ago, but his own physical therapy had kept him out of the loop for the most part. She'd changed little on the outside, but he knew the emotional toll had been high.

"Wow...she's grown up so much." He knelt down next to the car seat where Mia slept, with her chubby fingers wrapped tightly around a stuffed orange giraffe. "She's adorable and so much bigger than the last time I saw her."

"That's what babies do. They tend to grow up. She turns one this month."

"It's hard to believe that much time has passed." He stood up and faced her again. "Griffin told me you were hit from behind. Are you sure you're fine?"

"Yes, though I've been told that your mother's on her way to check us out."

"We'll need to have your car looked at as well, and what about the phone you thought they might be using to track you?"

She pulled it out of her purse and handed the phone to him. "Maybe I'm just paranoid, but I saw something a while back on TV about apps that can be installed to track someone without their knowledge. I didn't want to take any chances."

"You did the right thing. I'll pass this on to Griffin and see if someone who works with their IT can look at it. And Gabby… I promise we're going to find out what's going on."

She nodded, but he didn't miss the fear in her eyes.

"Do you have any idea who's behind all of this?" he asked.

There was a long silence before she answered. "I think this has something to do with Will's death."

Liam worked to process the information,

surprised at her answer. "Will's death? He died in an explosion halfway around the world a year and a half ago. How can this be related?"

She shrugged. "I recently went through the rest of Will's footlocker. I found some letters he wrote that I'd never seen before. He was worried about something. What if it wasn't just another attack? What if it was just meant to look that way?"

"Wait a minute. You mean that someone— other than terrorists—wanted him dead?"

"I think he stumbled upon something illegal while he was over there. Will hinted that contractors where involved, but I think he was afraid of the repercussions without solid proof of what was going on. And whatever it was got him killed. Because when I start asking questions…" A tear streamed down her face. "Liam, I think they're after me."

TWO

Gabby watched Liam's face, worried about his reaction. She knew Will had been his closest friend. They'd lived in a war zone together, and in turn, they'd developed a bond that only soldiers understood. On top of that, Liam had been there the day Will died.

"I don't understand." His jaw tensed as he caught her gaze. "Why would someone come after you in connection with a soldier who died seven-thousand miles away in the Middle East. It doesn't make sense. Will never said anything to me."

"Maybe not, but that's what I need to find out. Because there is a connection. I decided to start asking a few questions about things Will told me in his letters, and not only was I sent a threatening text message to stop asking questions, but now this happens."

"You said he was looking into something. Something...illegal?"

"Yes, but unfortunately, he never gave specifics."

"Why wouldn't he have told me if something was going on at the base? We talked about everything."

"I don't know. But he was definitely looking into some illegal activities."

He wasn't totally buying her theory. She could tell by the look of doubt in his eyes and the frown on his lips. He and Will had been close. She got that. She also knew there were things Will told him that he would have never told her. And yet, for some reason, this was different.

"Tell me more about the letters," he said.

"After he died, there were things I never went through in his locker. I just...couldn't. I was four months pregnant, then suddenly a widow... I was overwhelmed. A few weeks ago, I decided it was time to go through his things. I found several letters Will never had a chance to send. Someone must have added them to his personal belongings. In them, his tone had changed. He was looking for proof that someone was defrauding the government."

"Contractors."

She nodded.

"Who have you spoken to?"

"I contacted several officers he worked under, hoping they might have answers."

"But there was nothing specific in what he wrote? No names?"

She shook her head. "I'll let you read through the letters, but the only name mentioned was Casada. Someone he seemed to trust. Will thought the man might have answers for some reason."

"James Casada. He was a contracted worker."

"I guess I was hoping since you were there you'd have some answers, too."

He walked toward the window and stared outside. The snow was picking up, making her doubly thankful she and Mia weren't still out there.

"I'd like to look at the letters if that's okay, but I don't have answers. I know that things have been hard since Will died." He turned back around to face her. "Losing Will was a horrible tragedy that neither of us will ever be able to forget."

"It was horrible, but what better way to silence someone? No one would ask questions. It would simply be another unfortunate loss that happens far too often."

"I also know how easy it is to keep searching for an explanation when someone dies."

Gabby felt a ball of anger begin to bubble inside her gut. Hadn't she spent the last year and a half trying to combat those feelings? Weekly counseling sessions with her pastor, dozens of books on grief, along with advice from half the people she ran into while she tried to work full-time and raise Mia.

"I'm not just looking for answers." She bit the edge of her tongue. Healing was raw and personal. She knew that. Knew how easy it was to snap back a response that she'd later regret. But you couldn't just throw out grief with the trash and expect everything to simply switch back to normal. Healing was a process and losing Will had changed her forever.

"I'm sorry." He stepped in front of her and rubbed the back of his neck. "All I meant was that nothing can change the fact that he's gone. We know how he died and digging for answers is just going to hurt more."

"Maybe. But then why did someone ransack my house and follow me here? This all has to be related."

"All I know for certain is that Will died in an ambush. We all knew our jobs were a risk, but it was a choice he made every day in order to serve his country."

"I understand that, but what if there was more involved? Because I believe there was."

She'd been around Liam enough to know he was far more methodical than impulsive. His questions weren't a dismissal of what she believed, but rather his way of working through a problem.

"Do you have his letters with you?" he asked.

"I'm not really sure why, but I've been carrying them around in my car. Now I'm glad I did."

"Do you think that's what the intruder was after?"

"It makes sense. The only problem is I don't know what they think is in them." She blew out a slow breath. "I thought maybe you'd see something I didn't."

Liam pulled out one of the chairs and sat down in it. "Will seemed distracted before he died. But to be honest, I thought it was because he was ready to get back home. It just seems odd he never mentioned something like this was going on."

She caught the fatigue in his eyes, making her second-guess her impulsive decision to come here. He had enough of a burden to carry without her adding to it. He might not have died in the explosion, but he carried the physical scars as reminders. Months of therapy had healed most of them, but she understood all too well that it was often what couldn't be seen that hurt the most.

"You know, I'm sorry," she said, taking a step back. "I shouldn't have come. I just thought maybe you'd spoken to him and that you might have some of the answers. But you don't know anything, so—"

"Gabby, no." He stood up and bridged the distance between them. "You did the right thing. Of course, I'll help. I'll do anything I can, but in the meantime, I want to get you somewhere safe. I'll take you up to the ranch. I've been staying there the past few weeks while waiting to get approved for active duty. You'll be safe there, and it will give us a safe place to figure things out."

She caught the sincerity in his voice, but that didn't sway her response. "I couldn't impose. I'll just stay at the hotel here in town. I can't just drop everything, either. I've got my job—"

"Forget it. My mother would never forgive me if I don't insist you come. And in fact…" Liam turned toward the woman who'd just stepped into the doorway of the room, wearing a flowered scrub top and matching pants. "You remember my mother."

"Of course. It's good to see you again, Mrs. O'Callaghan."

"Please call me Marci."

"Alright, but I'm sorry you had to come down here. I'm fine. Really."

The older woman set a small padded medical bag onto the table. "Even at low speeds, there can be issues with whiplash and back injuries after a car accident. It's not something you should play around with."

Liam shot Gabby a smile. "If I were you, I wouldn't argue with my mom."

Mia started fussing in the car seat.

"I'm sorry, but I've forgotten your baby's name," Marci said.

"Mia."

"That's a beautiful name. Liam…why don't you entertain Mia while I look at her mama. I'll check her over next."

Gabby glanced at Liam. "You don't mind?"

"Of course not."

She handed Liam Mia, her stuffed giraffe and a small tub of Cheerios.

"We'll just wait for your mama in the hallway, won't we, Mia?"

Gabby turned back to Liam's mother while he stepped out of the room.

"You said you didn't have any complaints?" Marci asked.

"Besides being chilled to the bone, I feel fine. It could have been so much worse."

"Any bruises or cuts that you noticed?"

"No. I've got a slight crick in my neck, but it honestly isn't bad enough to even take Tylenol."

"Any trouble moving it?"

Gabby turned her head to the right, then the left. "No. None at all."

"No pain or dizziness?"

"Nothing."

She glanced at the hallway where Liam was pretending the giraffe was an airplane. Mia laughed, all smiles.

"He's really good with her." Somehow, she'd expected Liam to shy away from kids, but apparently she had been wrong.

"Liam might be a soldier who's served on the battlefield, but he's always had a soft spot for kids."

Gabby smiled, filing that information away with what she already knew about him.

"What about your parents?" Marci asked, slowly moving her hand down Gabby's spine. "Do they live near you?"

"They did until about a month ago. They're used to wintering in Florida, and I insisted they go this year. They'll be back for the holidays and some skiing this winter."

"It's got to be tough, raising a child on your own."

"Thankfully, I'm a graphic designer and able

to work at home. And Mia's an easy baby. Most days anyway."

It had taken her a while to convince her parents to take their yearly winter in Florida, but for some reason, doing things on her own this winter had been an important step forward for her.

"At this point," Marci said, "I don't notice anything to be concerned about, but some injuries can take several days to show up, especially in your spine or neck. If you have any numbness, swelling, back pain or headaches, you need to let me know immediately."

"Thank you. I appreciate it."

"How old is Mia?"

"She turns one in a few days. I can hardly believe it."

"Seems like my boys were that age not too long ago, though that's not exactly true."

Gabby laughed.

"Do you have any brothers or sisters?" Marci asked.

"I'm an only child."

Mia threw her giraffe onto the floor and started fussing.

Liam made his way back over to them. "I think someone needs her mama."

"You're good with her, but she's getting

sleepy, and I have a feeling she won't be herself until she gets a proper nap."

Mia just nuzzled her head into Gabby's shoulder while Marci quickly checked her out.

"From what Griffin told me, the accident was very minor, but you'll still need to watch Mia for anything that seems off like vomiting, not sleeping and unusual crying. I'd also suggest you do a follow-up with your pediatrician when you get home."

"I will. Thank you."

"I was serious about coming out to the ranch for a few days," Liam said. "I can make sure you're safe, and it will give us time to figure out who hit you."

"Your family's already done so much. I couldn't impose. I could get a hotel tonight—"

"That's out of the question. Besides, we have plenty of room. Right, Mom?"

"He is right. You'd be more than welcome to stay with us."

Will had told her about the O'Callaghan family and their ranch that sat nestled beneath impressive views of Pikes Peak and surrounding mountains. From everything she'd heard, she knew the place would be stunning. But as much as she wanted someone like Liam to take care of her, if he didn't have the answers, she'd have to figure things out on her own.

"Besides, I'll bet you could use some time away," Liam said. "It's a beautiful place. And if you're up for it, I could take you riding tomorrow. The fresh air of the mountains always makes me feel better."

"That would be nice."

There was nothing she'd rather do than spend the day in the mountains, away from all of this, but that wasn't why she was here.

Liam caught her gaze. "We'll talk more later. Just come for now."

She glanced toward the door, hoping she'd made the right decision. Hoping whoever had hit her wouldn't be able to find her.

"I'm going to keep you safe, Gabby. I promise. Whoever's after you won't find you at the ranch."

"You can't promise that."

"Maybe not, but I can do everything in my power to make sure you're safe. Griffin's trying to find the person who hit you, but in the meantime, I think we should head out to the ranch."

"If you're sure."

"I am." He reached out and squeezed her hand. "We're going to figure out what's going on. But first you need to get a good night's sleep. You look exhausted."

She let out a low chuckle. "Thanks."

"I didn't mean it that way."

"I know."

His smile managed to break through some of the pain in her heart. She could trust him. She had to. What other choice did she have?

The next morning, Liam sat out on the wraparound porch of his parents' ranch house, nursing a cup of coffee and watching the sun rise over the mountains. As beautiful as the scenery was, he couldn't shed the worry that had settled in his gut. He still needed to read Will's letters, but even if his friend had discovered corruption within one of the contracted firms, that didn't mean he'd been murdered. But then how did that explain the threatening text, the break-in and car wreck?

Had Will's death really been the perfect cover-up?

He shifted his thoughts back to the view. The O'Callaghan ranch had been his home his entire life and in his family's possession since the early 1920s. The thousands of acres included irrigated meadows, pastures, ponds for fishing and livestock. On top of that, there was some of the best elk hunting in the country. When he'd been deployed overseas, what he'd missed most had been Sunday dinners, hunting with his father and three brothers, and white Christmases. Three things that he might be getting more regularly if the army didn't sign off on his going back to active duty.

He pushed away the reminder as Gabby stepped out onto the porch wearing her long red coat, a scarf and boots, and holding a mug of coffee.

"Good morning," he said, jumping up to straighten a cushion on the chair next to him. "I see you found the coffee?"

"Your mother found it for me, actually." She sat down next to him, then took a sip of her drink. "This is just what I needed this morning. And she insisted she'd listen for Mia while I enjoy the sunrise."

"How did you sleep?" he asked.

She shot him a smile before sitting down next to him. "Like a rock. Mia managed to only wake up once, and she's still sound asleep. I don't think I realized just how tired I was."

"I'm glad you slept. Both of you. Everything always seems better when you have a good night's rest behind you."

He wasn't going to tell her how little he'd slept last night. He'd tossed and turned while going over every conversation with Will he could remember, trying to figure out what he'd missed. If Will had stumbled on something that had gotten him killed, he should have at least been aware that there was a problem. Why hadn't his friend come to him?

He pulled her phone out of his pocket and handed it to her. "Griffin dropped by earlier this morning and asked me to give it back to you."

"Did they find something on it?"

He hesitated. "There was spy software installed."

"Spy software?" Gabby let out a sharp puff of air. "How could they do that without physical access to my phone?"

"It's clean now, but apparently it is possible to install it remotely through a cellular or Bluetooth connection. Griffin's guy installed a security app to protect it from now on."

"Thank you. I just… I'm having a hard time processing all of this."

"I don't blame you. I am, too."

Gabby slipped the phone into her coat pocket then stared at the tree line in the distance. "Will told me how much you loved this place and wanted us to come for a visit after the two of you were finished with your deployments. I knew it was beautiful, but all of this… the colors of the sunrise…the fall leaves…the mountains… This truly is stunning."

The house was surrounded by aspens that turned golden every fall, as well as blue spruce and Douglas firs. With the sun slipping above the horizon, he couldn't imagine a more peaceful setting. But even with the pull of family and home, a part of him had begun to feel antsy and ready to go back to active duty.

"There's a tributary from the lake called Wayward Creek that runs through the part of the property," he said, pointing to the left. "It's one of my favorite places. And no matter what you like to do, hunting, fishing, snowmobiling in the winter, hiking, you can do it here. We even go ice fishing when the ponds are frozen over."

"Ice fishing?" She pulled her mug of coffee against her. "While my parents love their Florida winters, I admit, I prefer the snow and the cold. Though I've never tried ice fishing. That might be a bit too cold, even for my blood."

"I should take you one day, though…though I'm sure you're going to be ready to get home as soon as we figure out what's going on." He quickly tried to backtrack his invitation, wondering why he'd said that. Gabby wasn't here on holiday. She was here because her life had been threatened. And that didn't include excursions with him out on the ranch. She needed his help, which meant he needed to stay focused.

"What's the likelihood of falling through

the ice?" she asked. "I think that would be my biggest fear."

He shifted his mind back to the conversation. "My father taught us the importance of both having fun and being safe. But it happens. As long as you check your safety equipment and have the necessary gear in case of an emergency, you should be fine. Though my brother Reid fell in one winter while we were playing a game of hockey with skates, sticks and pucks. Took all three of us to drag him out, and we never told my father. We'd been lectured on the dangers of playing on the ice, and we knew he'd be furious."

Gabby laughed. "Somehow, I have a feeling that the four O'Callaghan brothers managed to get into a lot of trouble growing up."

"Well, we learned our lesson that time. We dragged him back to the house, stuck him in front of the fireplace and made him drink about a gallon of hot coffee. The only real issue after that was that he didn't sleep that night from all the caffeine, but we were just grateful he was okay."

He'd realized just how close they'd been to losing Reid, which was why he'd always believed God had stepped in that night. He glanced at Gabby. She'd pulled her long dark hair back in a ponytail and for the first time since she arrived, she looked relaxed. But what if he wasn't able to keep her safe? There were no guarantees in life. Hadn't he learned that the hard way? Reid had survived that day out on the ice. But on the battlefield, Will hadn't. If someone was after Gabby, how was Liam supposed to stop them?

He took a sip of his coffee, wishing he could somehow drown his worries. His training had taught him how to fight and how to survive, but it had never completely prepared him for what it was like to watch someone you cared about die. The emotional wounds he'd suffered had ended up being far worse than the physical ones he'd received.

She reached out and brushed her hand against his arm. "Thank you for bringing me here."

"It's not a problem at all. My mom's always telling us there's too much testosterone when we're all home, though I know she loves every minute of it."

"I'm sure she does. How often do the O'Callaghan brothers get to all be home at the same time?"

"Except for yours truly, pretty often, actually. You know Griffin. He's the oldest and one of the deputies in town, so he's around a lot. Next in line is Caden, who was an army ranger until he was honorably discharged three years ago. He now runs the ranch with my father and lives in a small house next to my parents' home. Reid's one of three full-time firemen in Timber Falls and lives there, and I'm the youngest."

"I don't think I knew that."

"The baby of the family, as they like to constantly remind me. I'm the one who's spent the most time away, but no matter where we are, we all always manage to find ourselves back at the ranch."

"I like your parents."

"My father considers retiring every year, though something tells me he never will. At least not officially."

She let out a low laugh, but her smile quickly faded.

"You okay?"

"For now, yes. It's almost too easy to forget the reason why I'm here." She pulled a handful of letters out of her pocket. "But as much as I'd love to just enjoy the sunrise, I need you to look at these."

"You're sure you don't mind?" Part of him felt uncomfortable reading through Will's personal letters to his wife.

"It's fine. I've organized them in chronological order."

Liam pulled out the first letter in the stack. "I used to tease Will for sending as many handwritten letters as emails. And do you know what his answer was?"

"That I loved handwritten mail?"

He nodded.

Gabby let out a sharp breath of air. "Now I can't help but wonder if it was also a way to write out his concerns without leaving a digital trail."

He started through the letters in order by date, surprised at how many memories they evoked. If he closed his eyes, he was there again, catching Will writing letters to his wife by flashlight in the tent in the middle of the night.

Why didn't Will tell me what was going on?

Twenty minutes later, he set down the last letter. "While my mom's watching Mia, would you like to go for a short walk? The fresh air always clears my mind and helps me think better."

She nodded, and they started down the path that led east of the house toward the creek, the reality of why she was really here at the forefront of his mind. Even with the idyllic scene of the red barn in the background and several horses in the corral, he couldn't ignore it. Someone had broken into her home, then tried to run her off the road. She needed answers and he was determined to get them for her.

"You were right. Will clearly stumbled onto something and didn't know what to do, but with no specifics, it's hard to know where to start. And just because he was tracking down some corruption doesn't mean he was killed over it."

"When I married Will, I thought I knew what I was getting into, but the reality is that you're never ready for long deployments and so many months apart," she said. "It was hard, but we were determined to make it work. In the back of my mind, I always knew that losing him was a possibility. What he did was dangerous, and I accepted that, but now... I guess having Mia makes me look at things differently. And this... I have no idea how to deal with this."

"There are a lot of things that you simply can't completely prepare yourself for."

Like losing someone you love.

"What did you think about the letters? What am I supposed to do?"

The phone he'd just given her back started dinging, and she pulled it out of her pocket to check her messages. A moment later, her face paled.

"Gabby...what's wrong?"

"It's a bunch of photos." Her voice broke as she spoke. "Liam…"

"Photos of what?"

She handed him the phone. There were half a dozen photos of her and Mia, snapped at several different locations. And after the photos was a chilling message.

We told you to stop asking questions. We know where you are. Don't go to the police. You will regret it.

THREE

Gabby spun around and started down the path back toward the house, her heart pounding. "I can't stay here. If they know where I am—"

"Wait a minute." Liam ran to catch up with her. "Look again at the photos. Where were these taken?"

"I don't know." She stopped, tears welling in her eyes as she pulled open the photos again. "In front of my house...the grocery store with Mia...getting into my car...it looks like the gym parking lot."

"They were following you. That is clear, but there are no photos of Timber Falls or the ranch."

Her brow narrowed in surprise. "You're right."

He took her hand and caught her gaze. "I think they're bluffing, because they don't know where you are. If they did, they'd show up here, not just send you photos."

"Maybe, but I still don't understand any of this." She worked to hold back the dam of tears about to break loose. "If they've been following me back home, why didn't they confront me then?"

"I don't know. Maybe they wanted to make sure you knew something before they did anything. This all began after you started asking questions."

"Yes."

"So it makes sense that someone's trying to find out what you know. And in the process scaring you to make sure you don't go to the authorities."

"Well, I am scared." She could hear the panic in her own voice but at this point, she didn't care. "Will is dead, and I have a child to protect. If anything happens to Mia, I'll never forgive myself."

Liam pulled her against him. "Nothing's going to happen, Gabby. Not to Mia. Not to you. I won't let it."

She nestled her head into his shoulder as he wrapped his arms around her. There was something calming in the warmth of his embrace. Something that made her want to stay in this moment for as long as possible. She missed feeling secure and cherished. Missed having someone to face life with. A partner for her. A father for Mia. Not that she was looking for someone to take Will's place. She was just so tired of doing everything on her own.

"I'm sorry." She pulled away from him abruptly and wiped her eyes. "I didn't mean to fall apart like that."

"You have nothing to be sorry about. You've been through a lot this past year and a half, and none of it's been easy."

"No, it hasn't, but my losing it isn't going to help put an end to all of this."

She started back to the house beside him. "I called James Casada two days ago. He lives in a suburb of Denver. Will indicated he trusted him. I thought it would be a good idea to talk to him in person. Maybe he knows something."

Liam stopped on the path and turned to her. "Did you get ahold of him?"

"Yes. He was out of town but was flying back to Denver last night. He told me he'd be working at home all day if I wanted to come by. I almost forgot I'd thought about going to go see him this morning."

"What if he's somehow involved in this?"

"You read the letters. Will trusted him and believed he could help."

"Which is what scares me. Someone thinks you have answers, and if they intend to silence you…"

"The problem is I don't really know anything."

"Maybe not, but someone thinks you do."

"I've gone over this in my head a hundred times. But you were there with him, Liam. You had to have seen something."

"Will worked some with Casada. Always spoke highly of him. And as I already told you, Will seemed preoccupied, but you were pregnant, and I thought he was just ready to get home." Liam shoved his hands into his pockets. "Is there anything else from Will in your house that might have answers about what he was working on, or maybe something they were after?"

"Not that I know of. But he had to have discovered something. Maybe someone is simply trying to guarantee that whatever they're involved in doesn't get found out."

"Let me go talk with Casada alone," Liam said. "See if he knows anything. You can stay here with Mia. You'll be safe."

"I can't just hide." While a part of her wished she could let him do this for her, she knew it was something she needed to do. "I've come so far in my search for closure over Will's death, but this... I need to find out what's going on. I need to talk to him myself."

They walked down the path flanked by aspen trees with gold leaves shimmering in the morning breeze, and the mountains rising up beyond them. She wanted to enjoy the scenery. Wished she could see God's hand in her own life as much as she saw it in the beauty around her. But instead, everything that had happened had left her with far more questions than answers. About loss. About fear. About God.

"But that said, my concern is for Mia." She broke the silence between them. "I can't do anything to put her life at risk."

"My mom's already volunteered if you need someone to watch her. If you feel comfortable."

"I do, but—"

"She's safe here. I promise. My dad will be here. Plus, it's Griffin's day off. He's promised to come by again later today and check on things."

"Okay." She drew a deep breath, wishing she felt as courageous about going to see Casada as she hoped she sounded. "Liam…thank you, but I still feel bad about getting you involved in this."

He shoved his hands into his pockets. "I haven't done anything really. And if Will were in my place, he'd do the same thing."

"I know, and while you might not know it, you've done so much for me. The times you've called me. Coming to see me when you weren't in therapy. The gifts for Mia. I owe you a lot."

And that wasn't all she owed him for. Now she'd dragged him into a dangerous situation. One she had no idea how to get out of on her own.

A wave of guilt shot through him. She was wrong. He should have called her more often. Made more of an effort to ensure that she and Mia had everything they needed. He couldn't imagine how difficult it had been for her as a single mom. He knew she'd been surrounded by her parents and friends and church family. Somehow that had allowed him to justify the times he hadn't picked up the phone to make sure she was okay. It had let him justify the fact that he'd been too busy with physical therapy. Too busy trying to get his own life back on track. But those had only been excuses.

He stared out over the mountains as they walked. Despite his desire to help her, what he really wanted was to leave the past where it belonged. In the past. Because while he didn't know what it was like to lose a spouse, he did know what it was like to lose a fellow soldier and best friend.

Having Gabby here was forcing him to remember things better left forgotten. But the past wasn't something that would simply disappear. He'd have to face it head on if they wanted to figure out what was going on.

An hour later, they were saying goodbye to his mother and Mia. He watched as Gabby held her daughter and smothered her with kisses while the little girl laughed. He handed Mia her giraffe, surprised when she threw it back at him. He held it out to her and she squealed as she grabbed it from him.

Liam smiled and snatched it back from her chubby fingers.

Mia laughed and lunged for him.

He grabbed her, surprised that she'd come to him so willingly.

She poked at his face with her finger. He responded by giving her a raspberry on her neck.

"We're never going to get out of here if the two of you keep playing." Gabby's tone was firm, but he didn't miss the twinkle in her eye.

He handed Mia to his mother. "We'll be back soon."

"She'll be fine." His mom settled Mia in on her hip. "Liam's father is here, so between him and Griffin you have nothing to worry about."

"I know." Gabby gave her daughter one more kiss. "Thank you."

They headed out toward his truck, while he prayed he was making the right decision.

Putting Gabby's life in jeopardy was the last thing he wanted to do. And yet, if they were going to figure out why she was a target, neither could they sit around and wait for the truth to emerge.

"Mia's adorable," he said, unlocking the vehicle and sliding into the driver's seat.

Gabby dropped her purse onto the floorboard, then buckled her seat belt. "She's the best thing that's happened to me. When I think I can't go on, she gives me a reason to get out of bed."

He glanced at her as he started down the narrow two-lane road toward town, suddenly wondering what it would be like to have a family of his own. Someone to share his life with. To laugh with. Someone who'd support him while he was deployed and be there for him when he returned.

He shoved away the random thoughts. Gabby was beautiful. There was no doubt about that. And he loved her passion and heart, but she was his best friend's wife. And even though Will was gone, there was way too much painful baggage between them to be anything more than simply friends. Still, something told him it would be far too easy for the lines of friendship and his concern for her to blur in his mind. Something he could never let happen.

"Do you remember anything more about James Casada?"

Gabby's question broke into his thoughts. "I wasn't around him much, but he always seemed honest and was a hard worker. I understand he was married at one time, but I believe his wife died a few years ago. That's part of the reason he was working overseas. He might have a couple adult children, but I'm not sure."

"Did you like him?"

"A lot of those contract guys are rough around the edges, but James was different. He seemed to be more like a...grandfather. Tough, but friendly, and he always had a story to share. He mainly worked in security for convoys that were carrying supplies between bases. A couple times, he was part of the detail that provided personal protection for the higher ups. And while he was six four and two-hundred-plus pounds, there was a gentleness to him that always took me off guard. I liked him. Everyone liked him as far as I know."

"Do you think Will would have wanted me to talk to him?"

"I don't know."

"But are we doing the right thing?"

He paused before answering her question. "What other choice do we have?"

Just over an hour and a half later, Liam

pulled in front of the house where James Casada lived. He'd enjoyed the drive through the mountains with Gabby, and the time to reconnect. But that's all this was. A couple of friends catching up. They'd talked about Will, he'd answered her questions about his rehabilitation and laughed at her stories about Mia, and he'd found himself surprised by how comfortable he felt with her. How much he enjoyed being around her.

"You ready for this?" He turned off the motor, then glanced at her.

"Yeah." She tugged on the end of her ponytail and nodded. "Let's go."

The yard in front of the one-story house had low maintenance ground cover and a few woody shrubs. Gabby rang the doorbell, then pulled her coat tighter around her. The sun was out, but the temperature had yet to climb out of the mid-thirties. A few seconds later, she rang the bell again.

"That's strange. He said he'd be here."

Liam glanced around the front of the house. There was no car in the drive, but Casada probably would have parked inside the garage. Nothing seemed off or out of place, but that didn't erase the uneasiness he felt. If the man knew something, he was a potential target as well.

"Mr. Casada?" Gabby tried the handle. "Liam, the door's open. Something's wrong."

He took a step forward. "Stay here."

"Liam—"

He squeezed her hand, then slowly opened the door. "James? Is everything okay? It's Liam O'Callaghan."

No answer.

Something was definitely wrong.

"If my phone was tapped. If they knew I was coming…"

A second later, Liam caught movement and turned. A figure rushed at him from behind the front door, slamming something into the back of his head. Stars exploding behind his eyes, he pivoted and swung at his attacker. But he couldn't fight the darkness sweeping through him as he collapsed onto the floor.

FOUR

Gabby heard her own scream as Liam slumped to the ground, but she couldn't move. A second armed man grabbed her, pinning her arms tightly behind her and pulling her backward toward the wall. She squirmed, trying desperately to get away, but his iron grip only tightened against her flesh.

A wave of nausea flooded through her. She glanced up at her attacker, and time seemed to momentarily freeze. Even with his ski mask, she could see his piercing brown eyes and the spiderweb tattoo on the side of his neck…

"You're such a fool." She could feel his breath against her ear as he spoke to her. "We already told you you'd regret nosing into something that's none of your business."

A shiver of terror coursed through her at his words. She'd ended up doing exactly what she'd promised herself she wouldn't do. Will had been a born warrior, sworn to obey and protect his country, and in the end, it had gotten him killed. What if coming here ended up putting her or her daughter in further danger? If these men had their way, the same thing was going to happen to her and Liam.

Her attacker gripped both her shoulders. "What do we do with them? If they really do have evidence—"

"She wouldn't be here if she'd found it."

"Maybe not, but this is going to lead back to us. That was never the plan."

Liam groaned on the floor as he struggled to get up. Sirens wailed in the background, shifting her gaze to the front window. Her attacker loosened his grip slightly at the distraction. She stomped on his foot with her boot, managed to jerk one arm away, then grabbed the lamp sitting on the end table beside her.

"Gabby!" Liam shouted her name. "Run."

Swinging with all her might, she slammed the lamp into her attacker's head. Glass shattered. Her attacker groaned, then stumbled backward, giving her the second she needed to pull away from him. She ran across the living room toward the one unblocked exit that she assumed led to the kitchen. She and Liam had no advantage against bullets. And she had no doubt the men intended to shoot them, which was probably what they'd done to Casada.

"We need to go," one of them shouted. "Now."

She stopped at the edge of the hardwood floor of the kitchen, then stumbled backward. James Casada lay still on the floor, eyes open and a gunshot wound through his forehead, blood trickling down the side of his face. But there wasn't time for regrets or grief. She glanced around the room for a cell phone.

A door slammed open, hitting the wall, and she spun around as Liam stepped into the room.

"Gabby…they're gone." Liam ran toward her. "Are you okay?"

"Yes, but…"

"Looks like they decided to cut their losses and run when they heard the sirens. And at least one of them will be leaving with a pretty good shiner."

She nodded, barely hearing him. Her legs were shaking. She felt as if she were going to throw up. How had this happened?

"He's dead." She turned back to Casada. "What if they come back?"

His hand squeezed her shoulder. "Are you okay?"

"No. They killed him." She pressed her hand against her mouth, biting back the bile. While Liam and Will had seen the terrors of war, the only dead bodies she'd ever seen had been faked on television, and even that was something she preferred to avoid. Give her a sappy romance movie any day over a cop show and reality TV. "They could have killed you…"

She fought to take in a deep breath, but the air wouldn't fill her lungs. She was responsible for this. If she'd never called Casada, never tried to involve him, he'd still be alive. And now she'd risked Liam's life on top of everything else.

"Gabby, the police are going to be here any moment now."

She looked up at him, her eyes wet with tears. "And you're bleeding."

He reached up and touched the side of his face. "It's nothing. I'll be fine."

Maybe he would, but she didn't think she'd ever be okay again. She needed to do something to fix everything that had just happened.

"Wait…" She grabbed a paper towel from the roll sitting on the counter, wet it at the sink, then started to dab at the blood, still unsure where the blood was coming from.

He took her hand to stop her. "I'm fine. We need to go out there now. Because while I'm not sure how we're going to explain what we're doing here, I'd rather not get caught hovering over a dead body."

She glanced toward the front entrance. Car

doors slammed. The police were here now, which meant they were finally safe. But if that was true, why did she feel so terrified? She dropped the paper towel into the trash, then followed Liam out the front door.

Officers were surrounding the house, their weapons drawn.

"Let me see your hands," one of the officers shouted at them. "Both of you. Now."

She raised her hands in the air, praying her legs wouldn't give out and willing her heart to stop racing. Her mind wanted to pray. To beg God to put an end to this, so she could go back to taking care of her little girl. But her heart wasn't sure He'd listen to her after all this time.

Two uniformed officers patted them down, searching for weapons, then combed through her bag.

"Let me see your ID."

Gabby slowly pulled her driver's license out of her wallet, then handed it to the officer.

"Liam O'Callaghan and Gabby Kensington." The officer turned to Liam. "You're military?"

"Captain Liam O'Callaghan. US Army."

"We received a 911 call that there had been gunshots coming from this house."

Liam nodded. "We came to visit the man who lives here. James Casada. I met him when

I was deployed in the Middle East. Two men were here in the house when we arrived. The door was open, so we went in, but he was already dead. The men fled when they heard your sirens."

A female officer approached them. "Their story fits. The neighbor across the street told 911 a couple matching their description showed up after she heard a gunshot and called 911. Said she was still on the phone with the operator when she saw two masked men escape down the street right before we showed up."

"Cordon off the house and get a BOLO out on the suspects. Turner and Sterling, go interview the neighbors." He turned back to them. "I'm Lieutenant Baxter with DPD. What can you tell us about the intruders?"

Liam shook his head. "Nothing as far as facial features. They both wore black ski masks. But I can give you a description of their clothes."

The lieutenant pulled out a notepad and pen.

"One wore khaki pants, a gray T-shirt and gray tennis shoes. The other one wore jeans and a black jean jacket and cowboy boots."

Gabby was amazed he remembered anything. In the middle of the attack, her mind had frozen and now any details she'd seen had vanished.

"Did you have physical contact with the men?"

Liam reached up and touched his face. "One of them hit me with something from behind before we even knew anyone was in the house."

"The paramedics just pulled up. I want you both checked out to ensure you're okay, then we're going to need a full statement from each of you."

A minute later, Gabby was answering questions from a paramedic, wondering how she'd managed having to be checked out by medical personnel twice in two days. "Miss Kensington? Does anything hurt?"

"I'll probably have a few bruises on my arms where he grabbed me, but that's all. I'm fine. Really."

Physically, at least. Emotionally was a whole different matter. She tried to concentrate as they ran through their list of questions and focused on her answers, but she couldn't settle her mind. These were no idle threats. Yesterday's accident made that clear. But did that mean they'd stumbled across the people who'd killed Will?

"Looks like you're okay, but it's probably a good idea to go to your own doctor for a thorough check-up, and if you need to talk to someone about what happened—"

"I will. Thank you."

She nodded. All she wanted to do was to get away from all of this and get back to the ranch and Mia. She sat on the curb outside Casada's house, her hands still shaking while the paramedics finished looking over Liam.

Everything seemed to move in slow motion around her. An officer yelled something across the front lawn. They were searching the house, trying to find the motivation behind what was going on. She pulled her phone out, needing to make sure Mia was okay, and called the number she'd programed into her phone for Liam's mom.

She let it ring until it switched to voice mail. "Marci…it's Gabby. I just needed to check on Mia and make sure everything is okay there. We've run into a bit of a snag on this end, so we might be gone longer than we planned. Just…just call me when you get this please."

She hung up, trying to convince herself there was nothing to worry about. Mia was fine. Glitches in cell phone service were common. Liam had told her that. If they'd gone for a walk or a drive, they wouldn't get her call. Which was okay. Liam's dad was there; plus, his brother Griffin had promised to stop by. And from what she knew about his family, you couldn't ask for better protection for her daughter.

She was just getting ready to try calling again when Liam climbed down from the back of the ambulance and joined her on the curb.

"You okay?" she asked.

"I've got a bit of a headache, but thankfully there's no need for stitches. What about you?"

"I'm fine, too."

"You don't sound okay."

She shot him a half smile. "You're the one with a goose egg on your head."

"I'm supposed to watch for any symptoms that might pop up, but they don't think it's a concussion. Just a nasty bump."

"I tried calling your mother but couldn't get through."

A flicker of concern registered in his eyes as he pulled out his phone. "I'm sure it's nothing. Signal out there can be spotty."

"I know."

"I'll give Griffin a call. Make sure the sheriff's office knows what happened here."

She grabbed the edge of Liam's sleeve, her adrenaline still racing, and leaned toward him. "But we can't tell them the real reason we're here. Not yet. This wasn't over. The text earlier told me not to talk to the police."

We know where you are.

Stop asking questions.

Don't go to the police.

You will regret it.

It was going to be a long time before she could forget the threats. A long time before she didn't see Casada's lifeless face staring up at her. All she cared about right now was protecting her child, and if it meant not telling the police everything, then it would have to be that way. Because she wasn't taking any chances.

Liam hesitated as he tried to form a response. While he understood her fears, figuring all this out on their own was no longer an option in his opinion. "I don't think we have a choice, Gabby. We need help to figure out what's going on. The authorities have the resources—"

"You're wrong. They threatened me again. In the house. Threatened Mia. I can't let them hurt her. Please. They said no cops, and if we go in there and tell those officers what happened I have no doubt that they'll follow through. The only reason we're alive right now is because a neighbor called 911 and spooked them, but this is far from over."

Which was exactly what had him worried.

"Then what are we supposed to tell the police?" he asked.

"Only what we have to. Casada was a friend of yours. We came by to visit him. That's all they need to know at this point. I want to keep Will out of this."

"And the fact that Casada's lying in the house with a gunshot wound to his head? How do we explain that? They're not going to just believe that our showing up when we did was a coincidence any more than I do."

"We came here to visit him, and he was already dead. Which they know. We were just paying an old friend a visit. There doesn't have to be anything more to our story."

Liam stared at his phone. "We need to find out the truth, Gabby, and I'm pretty sure that withholding evidence isn't the right way. How are we supposed to do this on our own? We don't even know what those men are looking for. And until we figure things out, you and Mia won't be safe."

"These people don't play games. We've both seen that firsthand now."

"All the more reason to tell the police what's going on. They need to know you've been threatened. You don't have to tell them everything, but we need to let them help us figure out what's going on."

She shook her head. "The men were searching the house."

"I know."

"They won't stop until they have what they

want. Until they ensure there is no one left to spill their secrets."

"I'll make a deal with you. We leave out Will's connection, for now, but you let me keep Griffin in the loop and see what he can find out. Quietly."

She hesitated before giving him an answer. "I'm not sure we should. Not yet."

"If you change your mind?"

"I'll tell you."

An hour later, they finishcd talking with the police. Gabby was exhausted. He could tell by the look in her eyes. He needed to get her back to the ranch where she could take a nap.

"We appreciate your cooperation in this matter," the lieutenant said. "We have your contact information and we will be in touch in case we end up with any more questions. All we need now is a signature on your statements and for you to double check that your contact information is correct."

Liam signed his name, then slid the paper back across the table to the officer. He hadn't lied. The only thing he hadn't mentioned was the threats Gabby had received and the possible connection to Will's death. He led Gabby outside to where his truck was parked, staying silent until they got into the vehicle.

She slid on her seat belt. "Thank you."

"I'm still not sure we did the right thing."

"They know enough. But there's something else I'm worried about. I've tried calling your mother three times now and no one answers. What about Griffin?"

He hesitated, knowing she wasn't going to like his answer. "I haven't got ahold of him yet, but I reached out to the Timber Falls sheriff's office. They said he was out on a call, and they'd have him get back to me as soon as possible."

He was positive it was nothing, but he wasn't sure she'd believe the same. She was scared and had every right to feel that way.

She was quiet as they took the highway south and headed out of Denver. He tried asking a few questions but finally gave up, realizing she wasn't in the mood for small talk. Instead, he used the scenic drive to come up with his own plan. He understood her fear of telling the authorities what was going on, but they needed help. Griffin could discreetly use his resources and try to find out about the men who'd attacked them, as well as James Casada.

"How's your headache?" she asked, breaking the silence between them.

"Better, thanks. Pretty much gone, in fact."

"I'm glad."

"Me, too." He glanced at her profile, wishing he could fix everything for her. "Gabby, what happened this morning was traumatic, and it's okay to feel scared."

"I know. I guess… I'm just more worried about Mia right now. She's totally dependent on me and yet I feel so helpless. Like there's nothing I can do to stop this. And that's what I'm supposed to do."

He knew that what had happened today had to have brought up a surge of emotions about losing Will. She was strong, but everyone had a breaking point. A place where they needed someone else to step in and help pick up the slack. But she also had a stubborn streak. Maybe that was a part of being a single mom when everything automatically fell on her. It had been a long time since she'd had someone to care for her and protect her. Which was exactly what he intended to do.

"I'd still like to read Griffin in on what's going on. Let him discreetly use the department's resources to see if he can find out who's behind this and keep us updated on the police investigation into Casada's murder."

He glanced at her, trying to gauge her reaction, but he couldn't tell what she was thinking. "Gabby?"

She nodded. "Okay. But only him for the moment."

"Agreed."

Liam's phone rang, and he pushed the answer button on the steering wheel.

"Mom?"

"I saw I missed a couple calls from you and Gabby."

"Yeah. We've been trying to get ahold of you."

"I'm sorry. We're fine. Your father needed to check on a couple fences, so we decided to take Mia with us. She loves the truck. I hope the two of you weren't worried."

"As long as you're all okay, that's all that matters. We're headed back to the ranch now, actually. I've got the call on Speaker."

"I just listened to your voice message, Gabby. What's going on?"

"We'll fill you in on everything once we get back to the ranch, but we're okay."

His mother had come to terms over the years with the fact that she had four adult sons who all had dangerous jobs. But he knew for a fact, as much as she tried to hide it, that it didn't mean she didn't worry. And she spent a lot of time on her knees in prayer.

"What about Griffin?" Liam asked. "Have you seen him? I've been trying to get ahold of him as well."

"He was out at the ranch with us until about an hour ago. He had to go out on a call."

"Okay. We'll meet you at the house shortly."

He hung up the call, then reached out and squeezed Gabby's hand. "Relieved?"

"Very."

"But?"

She let out a low laugh. "How did you know there was going to be a *but*?"

"Just a guess."

"I know I shouldn't let my mind automatically go to the worst-case scenario, but it's hard not to worry and question. Especially after all that's happened. I feel like I'm waiting for the next catastrophe to hit, and then praying I can deal with it." She stared out the window at the mountains in the distance. "Do you believe in prayer?"

"I do. I've seen enough horror in my life to know that without my faith I couldn't go on. But I've also learned that there are times when we feel like we're in the wilderness. When God's presence seems far away."

"And what happens when you can't find your way back? I believe God is out there. Know He still cares, but I've had a hard time praying these past few months."

"I've been exactly where you are and still too many times find myself there again. But Gabby, He's not out there, watching down on you from above. He wants His presence to be in you. Constantly with you. Even when things hurt the most. Maybe especially when things hurt the most."

The phone rang again, interrupting their conversation as Griffin's name showed up on the caller ID.

"It's my brother, but I'd like to continue this conversation."

She nodded as he picked up the call.

"Griffin? What's going on?"

"Sorry I missed you. Where are you?"

"Almost to Timber Falls, headed back to the ranch," Liam said, quickly filling him in on what had just happened.

"I hate to throw another wrench into the works," Griffin said, "but I need you to stop by town on your way. I've got some new information you're going to want to hear."

FIVE

Gabby stared across the sleepy diner on the outskirts of Timber Falls. At almost half past one, the lunch crowd had already headed back to work, leaving half a dozen empty tables.

Liam had tried to get her to order something, but she knew she couldn't eat despite the menu boasting comfort food. Her stomach was still tied up in knots, her adrenaline still racing. Even knowing that Mia was safe, and that Liam was determined not to let anything happen to either of them, she couldn't shake the lingering terror. It was the unknown that scared her the most. Not knowing who was behind this. Not knowing when or if they were going to strike, and how far they were willing to go. Becoming a single mom had changed the way she looked at everything. And it made it hard to let someone else in.

"Are you still okay with meeting with my

brother?" He picked up one of the cheese sticks he'd ordered.

She glanced at the door. "I want to get back to Mia as soon as possible, but I'm just as anxious as you are to find out what he knows."

"You can trust him."

"I know. I just…" She took a sip of the hot tea she'd ordered, hoping the drink would calm her nerves. "There is something that's bothering me."

"What's that?"

"Why didn't they just shoot us like they did Casada? They had every advantage. We were unarmed and they both had guns. And they certainly had the opportunity."

"To be honest, I thought the same thing, but I don't know."

"I get that they were spooked, but why run knowing we were probably going to end up talking to the police. Aren't we a liability?"

"They were masked, so they knew we couldn't identify them, and I'm also guessing they could be working for someone else. And here's another thing to throw into the mix." Liam wrapped his hands around his coffee mug. "I'm not a police detective, but what if they hadn't intended to kill Casada."

"What do you mean?"

"It seems to fit with their behavior. There

was an unopened box of donuts on the counter next to a set of car keys. They would have known Casada was home. Maybe their plan was to scare him into not talking to you, but then things went south when Casada fought back."

"That makes sense. I thought they could only track my location, but they had to know I was going to be there this morning."

"It's possible they were able to monitor your conversation and knew you were coming," Liam said.

She worked to put the pieces of the puzzle together in her own mind. "What about Will's death? How does it fit in then?"

"We still can't be sure at this point if his death was planned or simply an accident."

She jumped as the bell on the front door rang and a couple walked in. She shook her head. "Sorry."

He smiled at her. "For what?"

She held out her hands above the table. "I'm still shaking and jumping at every noise. My heart is racing and I... I just want this to be over."

"I know." He reached out and took her hands. "You're not the only one caught off balance. I might be military trained, but that doesn't mean this situation doesn't rattle me, too. The only thing I could think about was getting you out of there alive."

"I did. We both did."

The door jingled again, and this time she managed not to jump. Griffin stepped into the diner, but today he wasn't wearing his uniform. Instead, he had on jeans, a plaid shirt, and a tan jacket and boots, looking almost as handsome as Liam. And making her wonder why none of the O'Callaghan brothers had married. It was something she just might have to ask Liam if the subject ever came up.

Griffin slid into the booth where they sat in the back of the diner. "Are you two okay?"

"We are. And thanks for meeting us here and not at the station," Liam said.

"No problem." He glanced at Liam's appetizer plate.

Liam nodded at his brother. "Help yourself."

"Thanks, but I think I'll order something as well. I was planning to eat lunch at the ranch, but I got called out." He signaled the waitress and asked for a burger and fries.

Gabby just wanted to get to the point. "I'm assuming you found out something about my accident."

"I did, actually. But I'm not sure what to make of it."

"What do you mean?"

Griffin pulled a small plastic bag out of his pocket and laid it on the table.

"What is it?" Liam asked.

"It's a tracking device."

"Wait a minute... Where did you find it?" Gabby asked.

"On your car. I'm actually surprised we found it—it's so small—but the problem is this isn't some run-of-the-mill tracker you can buy off the internet. This one is military grade."

"They bugged my phone and my car?"

"I had our IT guy disable it, but yes." Griffin leaned forward. "You know I want to help, but I'm going to need to make sure I know everything that's going on."

Gabby glanced at Liam who nodded at her. He'd been right about one thing. She had to trust someone. "Besides the accident on the road coming here, there have been threats, both toward me and my daughter. I've been told not to go to the authorities."

"What do they want?"

"It started with a threatening text, then I showed up at my house yesterday and it had been trashed."

"What do you think they were looking for?"

"Evidence. Will had been following a paper

trail of some contractors he believed were defrauding the government."

"Have you seen the evidence?"

"No. Which is part of the problem. If Will did have evidence, I have no idea where it is."

"And yet someone believes she has it," Liam said.

"So, yesterday they run you off the road, because they were trying to scare you into giving it to them?" Griffin asked.

"That's my best guess."

"Tell me more about what happened in Denver?" Griffin asked, salting his fries. "How does your visit play into all of this?"

"We went to see a man by the name of James Casada," Liam said. "He worked with Will, and we believe he was someone Will trusted. His name was mentioned in one of Will's letters to Gabby. We were hoping he might have some information that would help."

"Did he?"

"When we got there, he'd been shot and the two men who killed him were in the house."

"I guess that would explain the knot on your head?"

Liam nodded. "You should see the other guy. He's got quite a shiner."

Griffin grabbed for a fry, then stopped. "If they were armed, how did you get away?"

"A neighbor called 911 after the first shots. The two guys ran as soon as they heard the sirens."

"Can you identify the men?"

"They were both wearing ski masks, so not their faces. I did give a description of their clothes to the officers, but that's all we've got."

"It's a start. What about you, Gabby? Did you notice anything?"

She waited to answer until after their waitress set down Griffin's burger and fries, and they reassured the woman they didn't need anything else.

"I wish I could remember something, but everything happened so fast."

"That's okay. You'd be surprised how many witnesses don't remember details after a trauma like that," Griffin said. "The only other new information I've got right now is the statement of a couple who saw the accident and called it in. While they didn't get a good look at the man in the vehicle, they did manage to get the model and color, along with a partial license plate, which we were able to track down."

"Did you identify the driver?" Liam asked.

"The car was stolen two nights ago."

"So another dead end."

"Unfortunately, yes."

"There's something else. It's just a theory, but what if their intentions weren't to kill Casada," Liam said, "but just to scare him, ensuring he didn't talk to Gabby?"

"And things got out of hand."

"Exactly," Liam said. "Their plan has definitely been to scare Gabby."

"And if they're convinced you have it, then they're going to want to make sure you are alive."

"I want to speak to the sheriff and get his opinion," Griffin said. "We'll keep this quiet, and I'll leave out the connection with your husband's death for now, but at some point it's going to come up."

Gabby nodded. "I just want to keep my daughter safe. That's all that matters."

Liam nodded. "And that's exactly what we're going to do."

"Why don't the two of you head back to the ranch now," Griffin said, sliding out of his seat. "And in the meantime, I'll see what I can do from this end."

"I know you're ready to get back to active duty, but do you know how much I'm enjoying having boots in the house?"

Liam glanced past his mom at the row of shoes lined up in the mudroom adjoining the kitchen, including his army boots, then smiled back at her. The house still smelled like cookies and hot chocolate like when he was a kid, and he was certain his mom hadn't aged a day. It had been the perfect place for four boys to grow up. The perfect childhood.

"Even though I'm anxious to go back," Liam said, dropping the dish towel onto the rack, "I've enjoyed every minute back on the ranch with you and Dad."

"A mother always knows that one day her children are going to fly the nest, but as proud of each one of you as I am, I can't help but wish every now and then that you had boring desk jobs that didn't include risking your lives."

He gave his mom a hug. "You raised us well and deserve some of the credit. Don't forget that."

"Oh, I take all of the credit." She laughed, then her gaze shifted to the staircase. "How is Gabby doing?"

"Okay, I think. I was just going to go check on her. I've been waiting, hoping she finally fell asleep. She's exhausted."

"Why don't you take her a few of these oatmeal cookies in case she hasn't fallen asleep yet." She grabbed a small plate from the cupboard, then started filling it with a few cookies from the cooling rack. "I made them for your father for after dinner, but he won't mind sharing. I don't think she ever ate lunch."

"As long as he won't mind sharing with me, too." Liam grabbed one and took a bite.

"Tell her I'll have dinner ready about six-thirty. Chili and corn bread." She shot him a wide grin. "Which means you'd better not spoil your dinner."

"Don't worry, I'll have room for both."

"You know, Liam…"

He waited for his mother to continue.

"She's the kind of girl I always pictured for you. She's pretty, smart and that baby of hers… Well, I'm a bit smitten. I'd forgotten how wonderful it was to have a baby in the house. It's been so long."

Liam frowned. "Let's not go there, Mom. Please."

"In case you forgot, I'm your mom and I can go anywhere I please."

He glanced at the bar stool. "Do I need to sit down for this conversation?"

"Funny. All I'm saying is that I'd like a grandchild or two, and don't think that's asking too much."

"In case *you've* forgotten, I'm the baby of the family with three older and very eligible brothers. Why don't you go talk to them?"

"Who are, unfortunately, at the moment all very single."

"That's not my fault."

"Of course not, but there's a beautiful young woman upstairs who thinks the world of you. And as for you… You feel something toward her, don't you? There's this something in your eyes when you look at her."

"There's nothing in my eyes, Mom. She's my best friend's wife. I'm worried and plan to ensure nothing happens to her, but that's it."

"She *was* your best friend's wife. Second love can be just as beautiful if you give your heart a chance."

If he were honest, he wasn't sure why none of the O'Callaghan brothers had tied the knot. It wasn't as if they hadn't come close. Caden had been engaged a few years ago, and at one time Liam had thought Reid would get married, but so far none of them had made it to the altar. A fact their mother was always quick to point out.

"Liam…you okay?"

"Yeah." He leaned down and kissed his mom on the forehead before grabbing the plate of cookies. "I'm going to check on her and, in the meantime, forget we had this conversation."

"Do what you want, but remember I want to enjoy my grandchildren while I'm still young."

He chuckled as he headed up the stairs.

Gabby's door was open, and she was sitting next to the bed in an overstuffed chair reading. He leaned against the door frame. "Hey... sorry to bother you. Is Mia finally sleeping?"

"Hey...yeah. She must have been completely wound up to where she couldn't settle down, but she finally crashed about fifteen minutes ago."

"Sounds like she had a good time with my mom and dad."

"She did. Your parents are amazing with her."

"I'd say it's the other way around. She has them wrapped around her finger. But you should take a nap as well. It's still early."

"I thought about it but I'm worried I wouldn't be able to sleep tonight."

He glanced down at the plate he was carrying. "Mom wanted me to bring you some of her homemade cookies. She's making chili for dinner, but we won't eat for a couple hours."

She folded her arms across her chest. "You and your family have done so much for me. I hope you know how grateful I am."

There were a couple bags he hadn't noticed at first lined up at the edge of the bed. Mia's diaper bag, Gabby's purse, the leather satchel. "Looks like you're going somewhere."

"Griffin told me my car had been checked over and it's drivable." She walked across the room. "I know you're not going to like this, but I've made a decision. Mia and I are leaving first thing in the morning."

"Wait a minute… Do you really think that's a good idea?"

"Talking with Griffin just confirmed how I've been feeling. Besides the fact that there are things I need from my house, you've done enough for me, and I can't ask you to fix this."

"In case you forgot, I'm already involved. And I have no intention of just walking away. We can always send someone to get whatever you need."

"I can't risk you and your family's lives. This isn't your battle."

He motioned for her to follow him out of the room, worried about waking the baby, then sat down in the sitting room in front of the large window overlooking the mountains. "I'm sorry, but your leaving isn't an option. Until we figure out what those guys are after, it's not safe for you to leave."

She sat down next to him on the edge of the seat. "I've got some money saved away. I can go—"

"Go where? Maybe this isn't any of my business, but you need to involve someone in this.

You don't want the authorities to know about the connection to Will, and that I get, but don't push me away."

Her gaze dropped. "I can't stay."

"Gabby, stop. Please. You're not making any sense. I can't let you leave."

"Can't or won't? This isn't your battle to fight. I never should have involved you in this."

He tried to curb his frustration. "You're wrong, and you're being ridiculous."

Her eyes widened. "Ridiculous?"

"Will was my friend. I should have seen that something was going on, but I didn't. Don't you understand that I want resolution for this as much as you do?"

"It doesn't matter. I've made my decision."

"You're being stubborn. I know when Will died, you took on a heavy load. You were suddenly a single mom with bills to pay and a daughter to care for. But as strong as you are, you're not thinking straight. You can't live on the run. Where are you going to go?"

"I don't know. I don't want to involve my parents, but as long as I have a computer and an internet connection, I can work anywhere. I'll figure it out."

"Don't do this, Gabby."

She shook her head. "You don't understand. No matter how hard I tried to prepare myself, when those officers came to my door and told me that Will was dead, it was like my world ended. I felt that everything we'd dreamed of together was gone. And now, just when I finally feel as if I'm escaping the fog, someone's threatening my daughter. I can't just sit here and wait for things to be resolved."

He ran his hand down her arm, searching for the words to convince her she had to stay. "We're not just going to sit here. We're going to figure out who these guys are. And we're going to find out what Will died for."

Silence hung between them as she blinked back the tears.

"Please stay," he said. "I'm asking you to stay and let me help. You don't have to do this alone."

Her shoulders dropped as if she were starting to give in. "I feel like I've been doing this alone for a long time. Living on my own. Making my own decisions. Fixing my own problems."

"What about your church family? Have they been there for you?"

"They have. Especially at the beginning, but you know how it goes. Time passes. I'm no longer a couple, and it's harder to fit in now. People moved on. And I can't really blame them. They have their own lives to lead."

"I know Will struggled with his faith at times," Liam said. "He was strong, but you were always his anchor. Spiritually. Emotionally."

The tears started to fall, making him hate to see her hurt like this.

"I've tried not to let it happen," she said, "but when Will died, I felt so alone. I never blamed God, not really, but somehow in the process I just…stopped praying. Stopped feeling His presence. And while I've made progress, I feel like I'm getting pushed back into that place again where I don't want to go."

"Then don't, Gabby. Stay here with my family. You need to be surrounded by people who care about you. Not running. And what about Mia? If you want to protect her, you certainly don't need to be on your own."

She glanced out the window at the cloudless sky. "I'm sorry."

"For what?" he asked. "For feeling? For caring? Don't try to close yourself off."

"I just… I don't know how to do this."

"I know I can't understand what it's like to lose a spouse. But I lost a friend…and I still might have lost a career. I know what it's like to feel helpless and uncertain."

She grabbed a tissue from the coffee table

next to her and blew her nose. "Maybe we do need each other."

"I think you're right." He smiled, trying to ignore the stirring of his heart, as he had ever since she'd shown up. "Don't make any decisions now. I promise everything will seem better tomorrow. Okay?"

She looked up at him with those big dark eyes of hers, pulling his heart toward a place he wasn't ready to go.

"Okay."

"Just promise me you'll stay here for now."

She reached up and grasped his hand, letting him pull her up. Sunlight streamed across the shimmering aspen trees in the distance. "It's beautiful, isn't it?"

"Stunning."

"When I'm looking out there, I know God's here," she said. "I can feel His presence. I just have to find a way to completely trust Him."

He brushed her hair behind her shoulder. "Promise you won't go running off in the night?"

She nodded. "I promise."

SIX

Gabby watched Mia squeal as she grabbed the last piece of banana off the high-chair tray. "Do you want some more banana?"

Mia gave her one big nod. "Peez."

Gabby laughed.

Liam grabbed another banana from the counter, then crouched down in front of Mia. "Aren't you getting sleepy?"

She shook her head at him.

"Of course not."

"She took a long nap. Maybe too long," Gabby said.

Liam's father Jacob stepped into the room with a big grin on his face. "And perhaps she's a bit spoiled by my wife."

"You can blame me." Marci grabbed a cookie from the plate at the center of the table. "But since my darling boys have yet to give me grandbabies, I claim my right to enjoy Mia while she's here. As you can see, I've even kept in storage the high chair, crib and a few toys from when my boys were little, simply in anticipation of those grandbabies."

"I know my parents would agree with you. They love being grandparents," Gabby said.

Liam laughed. "Please don't get her started."

The back door opened. "Anyone home?"

"Griffin, Caden… I was hoping you boys would make it. There's chili on the stove if you're hungry."

"I'd love some, actually." Griffin glanced at Gabby. "How are you doing?"

"I'm good. Especially with all your mom's cooking."

"You really know how to win extra brownie points with my wife, though no one would argue with you." Jacob grabbed a couple more chairs for the brothers. "Why do you think I've gained forty pounds over the course of our marriage?"

Marci winked at him. "You're as fit as the day I met you, and twice as handsome."

"Just a bit more of me to love now, but talk about brownie points."

"You remember Caden, don't you, Gabby?" Liam pointed to his brother as he sat down in one of the chairs.

"Yes. It's good to see you again."

"It is," Caden said, "though from the little I've heard from Griffin, this hasn't exactly been a restful visit."

"No, it hasn't," Gabby said. "Any news?"

"There is, actually," Griffin said. "I've been in contact with the authorities in Denver."

"And…"

"They told me that Casada died instantly from the gunshot. And they found a second gun and a second bullet in the wall."

Gabby glanced at Griffin. "What does that mean?"

"They think Casada shot at the intruders but missed. And here's something else." He thanked his mom for the bowl of chili, then slid into the empty chair. "We were able to identify the men who ran you off the road."

"How did you do that?" Gabby asked.

"We have a new program in the county where we encourage residents and businesses to register any security systems that record public areas. It enables us to quickly access camera footage that might in turn give us information on crimes. There was a gas station camera that caught footage of them in the stolen vehicle."

"Who are they?"

"Kyle Thatcher and Silas Maldin. We don't know anything about Maldin at the moment, but Thatcher has been in and out of jail, always on small-time stuff. He was discharged from the army about three years ago. I'm still waiting for those records."

"Sounds like an all-around good guy," Liam said. "Have you found either of them?"

"Not yet, but we will." Griffin pulled up a photo on his phone, then set it in front of them. "Do either of them look familiar?"

"Wait a minute. Maybe." Gabby picked up the phone. A memory surfaced. "What's that on his neck?"

"It's a tattoo. That's Thatcher."

"That's the guy that pinned back my arms inside Casada's house. I'm sure of it. I couldn't remember any details when we talked to the police, but he had that same tattoo."

Griffin nodded. "That's good. Very good. Because that means we can definitely connect the two cases. We've got a BOLO out for him. We'll find him."

Liam grabbed another slice of corn bread and started buttering it. "There's got to be a connection between the army and the tracking device."

"Agreed," Griffin said.

"Gabby asked me to read through Will's letters," Liam said, "to see if there's something I might be able to find that she missed. I've started reading them again and taking notes.

Everything that might be related to what he was looking into. If it's alright with Gabby, I'll email you my notes on what might be relevant."

Gabby nodded. "That's fine with me."

"I think that's a good idea," Griffin said. "And in the meantime, I'll do some more digging into Kyle Thatcher and his connection to all of this while we try to find out something about Maldin."

Their voices faded as they discussed the situation. She'd never imagined things could have progressed this far. A man dead. Someone threatening her and her daughter.

She suddenly felt hot. Memories she'd managed to suppress over the past few months engulfed her. Memories she didn't want to relive. The knock on the door to inform her Will was dead. His funeral. And then today, Casada's dead body on the kitchen floor.

Mia started fussing. Gabby handed her another piece of banana, but she couldn't think. Couldn't breathe. She needed some air.

She rested her hand on Marci's shoulder. "Would you mind watching Mia for a minute? I'll be right back."

"Of course. Are you okay?"

"Yeah. I'm fine."

She hurried outside onto the front porch,

then immediately wished she'd thought to grab her coat. But she couldn't go back inside. Not yet. Instead, she braced her hands against the railing and stared out across the shadowy outlines of the ranch and the canopy of stars above her.

"I know You're there, God, and I really want to trust You."

She prayed out loud, hoping that would somehow make God hear her better. Which seemed foolish. If God could create the stars and the mountain ranges surrounding her, did she really doubt He could hear her small voice?

She bit back the tears. "I want my faith to be strong like it used to be. Strong enough that it's isn't choked out by fear and anxiety. But sometimes it's just so hard. Sometimes I just don't know how."

The screen door squeaked open.

"Hey…" Liam walked up beside her. "Are you okay? My family can get a bit rambunctious, which can be overwhelming if you're not used to it."

"It's not them. Really. And I'm the one who's sorry." She wiped away a tear and forced a smile. "I shouldn't have run out like that but hearing you all talking about Will… It all just dragged up a lot of memories I thought I was finally coming to peace with."

"I never meant to be insensitive." He grabbed a blanket from one of the chairs and set it around her shoulders. "None of us did."

"You're not. I promise."

She caught his profile in the soft light, surprised at how quickly he'd become an anchor in her life. He'd always been there for her, but from afar. Now he was here, with her. A place of calm and refuge in the middle of the storm. Something she'd been looking for without even knowing it was what she needed.

She lowered her gaze. "And you were right about something."

"What's that?"

"I've spent so much time taking care of Mia and myself on my own I've forgotten what it's like to have someone take care of me. You and your family have been amazing. I'm so grateful. Really. I want you to know that."

"Family's nice, and something I know I've taken for granted as well. Because you're not the only stubborn one in the bunch. After my accident, I hated having people help me with things I felt like I should be able to do. I fought and fought until one day I realized I needed those around me if I was going to make it. And that was okay."

She turned her attention back to the night sky. "It's a beautiful and clear tonight."

"Hard to believe there's a storm that's supposed to come through in a few hours. They're predicting snow by morning."

"I love the snow. My dad taught me to ski. It's funny, though, because now he's the one who wants to flee to Florida at the first sign of snow."

"Have you told them what's going on?"

She shook her head. "I need to, I know, but they worry about me. It took me weeks of convincing for them not to give up their winter in Florida. They're planning to be back in a few weeks for Christmas, but I guess I felt the need to prove I could do it on my own."

"You have nothing to prove. Nothing at all."

She turned back to him and caught his gaze. Her heart was racing, and her palms were sweating, but this time it wasn't from the anxiety of the situation. He was next to her, calming her fears, making her feel safe again. Making her feel as if she weren't alone anymore.

A noise at the end of the porch jerked her back to reality.

"Did you hear that?" she asked.

"Hear what?"

"I don't know. It sounded like there's something at the end of the house. If they're here…"

"We get quite a few wild animals that pass this way, but stay here. I'll go check it out."

She stood on the edge of the porch, the hairs on the back of her neck raised, from fear as much as from the cold. And added to that was the confusion of what she'd just felt with Liam next to her. But she couldn't go there. No matter how much she longed to feel safe again. Whatever feelings she thought she had weren't for the right reason. And she wouldn't do that to him. And on top of that she couldn't get involved with another soldier.

There was only one thing she needed to focus on right now and that was keeping Mia safe and finding a way to end this. Because as much as she trusted Liam, until the men who were behind this were in prison, she wasn't going to be able to stop searching for an answer to what was going on. Anything else was simply a distraction.

Another noise shifted her attention back toward the other side of the porch.

"It's just me," Liam said.

She frowned. "I can't shake this jumpiness. Did you find something?"

"No. There were no signs of anything out there."

It had probably been nothing more than a

fox or raccoon that she'd heard. She was letting her imagination run wild.

"You're going to think I'm completely paranoid."

"After all that's happened?" He let out a low laugh. "Hardly. Don't worry about it. I'd always rather be safe than sorry. Why don't we go back in? It's late, and you never got that nap. I know you're exhausted."

She stifled a yawn and nodded. "Maybe I'm more tired than I thought." She rested her hand on his arm for a moment. "Liam…thank you. For everything."

Her stomach flipped like she was eighteen again and a boy had just paid her a compliment. She had to ignore whatever was going on between them. Liam had been Will's best friend, and this was simply her feeling vulnerable. Nothing more. As soon as they found out the truth, she'd go back to her own life and he'd go back to his.

"You okay?" he asked.

"Yes. I think I'll head to bed like you suggested. I know Mia needs to go to sleep as well."

He smiled down at her. "We'll all feel better in the morning. Trust me."

Gabby woke with a start. Sweat beaded off her forehead and her pillow was damp. She'd had a nightmare. Like the ones she'd had after Will had died. They left her feeling like the walls of her room were closing in around her, as if it were happening all over again. She grabbed her cell phone from the bedside table and checked the time. It was only three in the morning.

She pulled back the sheets and crossed the room to check on Mia. Moonlight filtered through the window's sheer curtain. Her daughter's tiny fingers were wrapped around her giraffe, a hint of a smile on her face. Perfect. Peaceful. That was how Gabby needed to keep things for her.

She dropped the intercom receiver in the pocket of her robe, then headed toward the kitchen. What did the Bible say about having the faith of a child? Mia was completely reliant on her for all of her needs. When was the last time Gabby had come to God with the faith of a child, giving up control and trusting in His promises?

Thank You for this sweet girl, God.

The words came automatically in the form of a prayer. She'd avoided praying for so long after her loss, and yet she'd missed that relationship she knew she needed. Liam was right. She had to find a way not to feel ashamed to ask for help and depend on others.

She grabbed a glass from the cupboard, filled it with water from the fridge, then took a sip. There was no way she should be hungry, but the plate of cookies sat on the counter and she took one.

Something crackled on the intercom. She reached for the receiver and caught someone's faint whisper. Panic swept through her as she dropped her glass into the sink and it shattered. She ran up the stairs, taking them two at a time and screamed as she stepped inside the room.

The bedroom window was open, the curtains floating in the breeze. Mia's crib was empty.

Liam heard a scream, then someone banging on his door. He glanced at the clock as he fought to pull himself out of the fog of sleep. It was just past three o'clock. The door opened, letting light from the hallway pour into the room. Gabby stood at the foot of his bed.

"Liam…hurry, please. It's Mia. Someone's taken her."

It only took a second for what Gabby said to register.

"Wait a minute… How's that possible?" He grabbed his cell phone from the side of the bed and headed out of the room with her, not fully awake.

"I went downstairs, heard something on

the baby monitor and when I came back she was gone."

He ran into the room where Gabby and Mia had been sleeping. The window had been forced open, bringing a cold draft into the room.

"How long?"

"A minute at the most."

"Which means they couldn't have gotten far."

"That's not all." Gabby grabbed his sleeve and handed him something. "They left a note. I've got twenty-four hours to give them the evidence, or I won't see Mia again."

"That's not going to happen."

His parents appeared in the doorway. "What's going on?"

He headed back down the hallway, shouting out instructions to call Caden and the ranch hands to the house as he dialed Griffin's number.

"Mia's gone," he said as soon as Griffin answered.

"What—"

"I don't have any answers yet, but we need to get a search team together and put out an AMBER Alert. I figure they've only got a couple minutes lead, so I've called in Caden and the ranch hands."

"Did you see who it was?"

"No, but this has to be connected."

"I'm on my way now."

"What do you want us to do?" his mom said as soon as he'd hung up the phone.

"We're going to need extra warm layers, flashlights and the radios. The temperature's already started dropping."

He headed outside as Caden and the three ranch hands arrived.

"I checked the barn on the way here," Caden said, following him to the side of the house where the men had to have accessed Gabby's bedroom. "Two of the horses are gone."

"Did you see any tracks?"

"There were some heading toward town, but they got lost in the tire tracks."

Liam's frustration grew. "It's supposed to start snowing soon, but right now the ground is still hard. Tracking them in the dark isn't going to be easy."

"If they're moving by horse, there are only a couple options out of here," Caden said.

"Agreed. We need to split up." Liam nodded at his brother. "Take one of the ranch hands and head toward town. Have the other two saddle up a horse for me, then head toward Wayward Creek and scout out the immediate terrain. I'll head up the mountain on the off chance they went that direction."

"By yourself?" Caden asked.

"I'll be fine. I think Dad should stay here with Mom and Gabby."

Caden nodded. "I have to agree with that."

"I'm coming with you."

Liam glanced up at the edge of the porch where Gabby stood. "I need you to stay here with my mom and dad. Keep the coffee hot and be our communication center. It's cold out and there's a storm scheduled to hit in the next couple hours. I don't want you out there."

She marched down the stairs.

He let out a huff of air, knowing what she was thinking. Temperatures were dropping, and Mia was out there with a couple of abductors who could care less about what happened to her. They would find her, but he didn't want Gabby caught in the crosshairs as well.

"Gabby—"

She stepped in front of him, already bundled up. "I'm going with you."

"Forget it."

"Please. You can't make me stay here in this house without doing something, and there's no time to argue. Every minute we spend here is another minute they're ahead."

He hesitated, but if he were honest with himself, he knew he'd do the same thing if he were in her place.

"Do you ride?" he asked.

"Since I was ten. I can keep up."

He pulled on his boots and layered up, including the wool cap and gloves his mom handed him, hurrying as fast as he could. They'd been watching. He was sure of that now. And he'd thought it was some wild animal.

But heaping himself with guilt wasn't going to help him find Mia. They needed to get out there. Now.

He passed out the radios to everyone.

"How are we going to find them in the dark?" Gabby asked, pulling her wool cap down over her ears.

"It will be slower going, but they have their own disadvantages that will slow them down as well."

Like Mia.

His dad handed Gabby a pair of gloves. "Part of Liam's military training was combat tracking and counter tracking. He knows what he's doing."

His mom squeezed Gabby's shoulder. "And Caden's a former army ranger. If anyone can find her, my boys can."

Liam caught her gaze. "She's right. We will

find her. There are only two ways out of here that would make any sense in the dark. The main road that leads to town and a well-worn trail that heads southeast through the forest. The terrain is more difficult, but definitely passable when there's no snow on the ground."

"What can I do?" his mom asked.

He turned and kissed his mom on the forehead. "Once they're done saddling the horses, have the ranch hands search the vicinity and see if they can pick up anything we miss. And have a big pot of coffee waiting when we get back."

He hurried to the barn with Gabby. Griffin and one of the ranch hands were already in the truck and heading out.

He quickly checked around the outside of the structure before heading inside. "Caden was right. There are horse tracks leading east toward town, but these guys are smart and will try to throw us off."

He quickly secured a saddle scabbard for his rifle on the side of the horse. The cold was already biting, but he couldn't worry about that now.

"You're riding out armed?" she asked.

"I have no plans of giving them any more advantages than they already have."

"It just never seems to end." She stood beside the second horse while the ranch hand got it ready for her. "This nightmare."

"I know you're scared, but we're going to find Mia. We're only a few minutes behind them and my brothers and I know this land better than anyone. They also have the disadvantage of it being dark. The four of us used to spend every minute we could exploring the ranch."

"But if they're trained soldiers as well—"

"We're going to find her."

He mounted his horse, praying at the same time that everything he was telling her was true. He couldn't even imagine how terrified she must be. But they were going to find the little girl. They had to.

"I know you don't know the terrain but keep up the best you can," he said, praying he wouldn't regret his decision to let her come. "We're going to have to move fast."

They headed south on the path, silence hovering between them. When he'd spent time training how to track the enemy, he never imagined having to track his best friend's daughter. But this was no different. If they were out there, he would find them. Which meant not only did he need to be aware of everything going on around him—any footprints, disturbed soil, trampled grass—he also needed to get into the head of the kidnappers. Figure out what their plan was.

If he were them, this is how he would have left. The easiest way out of here might be the road leading to town, but it also would be the riskiest and the easiest to get caught.

He glanced at Gabby, impressed with how she was keeping up. As much as he wasn't happy about risking her coming, he knew she was strong. He wasn't sure she saw it in herself, but he did. She'd managed to stay calm tonight. She hadn't gone into hysterics. Instead, she'd demanded to be a part of the search. Maybe she'd break down when this was all over, but for now she'd managed to find the inner strength that enabled her to cope.

"I'm pretty sure they went this way," he said. "There are two sets of hoofprints."

"Where does this path go?"

"It's a pass that leads toward Mountain Springs."

"And between here and there?"

"Nothing more than the forest, and a cabin a friend of mine owns."

He didn't want to tell her that the path would be covered in snow in the next few hours, making it harder to pass. And there were other things that bothered him since they'd left. He could out-track anyone he knew. The army had ensured that with his training. But if they were right about who had been hired, he was sure they'd come with their own set of skills. And they had to have equipment as well. The tracking device they'd used on Gabby's car wasn't something they could have picked up just anywhere.

He wasn't sure how they'd done it, but they must have planted another to find out exactly where Mia would be sleeping, and the exact moment Gabby would be gone. He was pretty sure they'd come through the window and not one of the other doors. It had been a plan well thought out and executed. Which was exactly what had Liam nervous. They weren't dealing with amateurs. Thatcher might have a shady past, but that didn't mean he wasn't well trained.

He heard something snap, then stopped, raising his hand for Gabby to be quiet.

Liam jumped down off his horse and listened for something out of place. He turned back around, staring out into the night toward where they'd come from. He heard it again— a subtle crunch.

Someone was behind them.

"Liam…"

"We're definitely on the trail of someone, but that's not all. We're also being tracked."

He scanned the darkness, trying to figure out what he'd missed. He'd been tracking two people. Where had the third come from? Or maybe that wasn't what was happening at all. Had one of the men looped around, trying to box them in? He searched the wooded forest, but the only thing he could see was tree limbs moving in the wind. The only light was from the moonlight, but as soon as the storm clouds came in, they wouldn't even have that.

He grabbed for his rifle from the scabbard, but it was too late. A gunshot ripped across the night. Gabby's horse bolted, throwing her to the ground.

SEVEN

Darkness closed in around her followed by an eruption of stars as Gabby hit the hard ground. Her mind fought to focus as she waited for the sound of another gunshot. Someone was out there. Close enough to fire shots at them. And Mia... She had to be with them, which terrified Gabby. She listened for the sounds of Mia crying, but all she could hear was the rush of wind around her. If Mia was somewhere nearby, she had to get up and find her.

"Gabby... Gabby talk to me."

She opened her eyes and stared up at Liam, who was framed in darkness with only a hint of moonlight allowing her to make out his features.

"Are you okay?" he asked.

"I think so."

"Move slowly, but you need to get up. We have to get out of here. Now."

She let him help her up, making sure as she

moved that nothing was broken. For the first time all night, she was thankful for the cover of darkness. But why shoot at them? So far, the men had seemed to want her alive. Liam put his arm around her and helped her to her feet. She stared down the path ahead of them, but darkness made navigating the terrain almost impossible. If it wasn't for Liam and his training, they'd never have made it this far.

"Why did he shoot at us?"

Liam was guiding her down a smaller trail that deviated away from the main path, keeping his arms around her as they hurried through the icy darkness.

"Maybe he was trying to slow us down. I don't know."

She glanced around her as another realization hit her foggy mind. "Where are the horses?"

"They were spooked by the gunshot and ran. I managed to grab my rifle, but that's it."

"So what do we do now?"

"We're going to have to walk out of here."

She heard the anger in his voice. The cold felt like a knife through her lungs as she took in a deep breath, trying to settle her nerves. They'd been traveling on horseback for a couple hours, but now that it had started to snow, the terrain was going to be even tougher to cross. If they turned back to the ranch, it would take even longer. She had no idea what was out there. Only that trusting Liam was her last hope now.

The realization left her feeling vulnerable. Out of control. And she hated feeling out of control.

She glanced back through the eerily shadowed forest. "Do you think he's behind us?"

"He's out there, but I don't think he's coming after us."

"Which leaves us where?"

"There's a cabin south of here off the main path. The one I mentioned earlier that belongs to a friend. It will be a lot quicker to reach that than heading back to the ranch. The man who lives there should have a way for us to warm up."

She zipped her coat up a couple inches, then wrapped her scarf around her neck a second time. They pressed through the trees in silence. She forced herself to keep up with his pace, trying to follow in his footsteps so she made as little sound as possible. Night sounds echoed around her. She shivered, both from the cold and from the fear that had settled in her gut. They were out there. The men who had broken into her house...killed Casada... kidnapped her daughter.

Where are you, Mia? Mama will find you. I promise.

Her lungs were burning, and she didn't know if it was the altitude, the fall or both, but either way she needed to stop and catch her breath.

She stood in the middle of the trail and turned to Liam. "I just need a minute."

"Of course. How are you feeling? How's your head?"

"It's sore, but fine. I just need to catch my breath."

He led her to a flat rock on the side of the trail. "Rest here. I'm going to try and radio my brother."

An owl hooted in the distance. An ensemble of insects chirped, even in the cold.

"I can't get through." He knelt in front of her. "Tell me how you're really feeling. Do you feel nauseated or dizzy? You took quite a blow back there falling off that horse."

"I really do think I'm fine, though the back of my head hurts. I'm pretty sure I'm going to end up with a lovely goose egg."

He shot her a smile. "Trying to compete with me, huh?"

"Funny, because I'd have been perfectly happy to have skipped this drama. Do you know where we are?"

"More or less. Not sticking to the main trail

is going to make it harder, but this is a short-cut to the cabin."

"I'm slowing you down."

"You're fine, and besides…you're definitely much better company than my brothers used to be when we played hide-and-seek out here. We'd spend half our time arguing about who was the best tracker, or the best aim."

"Let me guess. You were the best tracker out of the four of you?"

"My brothers would never agree with that statement, but I was pretty good. Their problem was they couldn't go more than a minute without talking or making some kind of noise. I loved tracking, even back then."

She glanced toward the east where a hint of light was already breaking above the horizon. "It's going to be light soon."

"We will find them. There's nowhere they can escape. We'll figure out how to let my brothers know where we are. The cabin's not too far now."

She nodded, wanting to believe him, and yet whoever had taken Mia still had the advantage.

He caught her gaze in the soft glow of dawn. "You're shivering."

He sat down next to her and wrapped his arm around her waist, letting her burrow her head into his shoulder. He took her gloved hands and rubbed them between his, trying to warm her up. She was so cold. They were dressed for the weather, but losing the horses put them at a huge disadvantage. Besides that, they had no access to water and food. They needed to get somewhere safe and warm, but at the moment all that mattered was finding Mia.

A branch creaked overhead while the wind whipped around them. Her head throbbed, but she couldn't focus on that. His warm breath tickled a small exposed place on her neck. And with his arms around her, she finally felt as though she were warming up.

"When I found out Will was dead, I felt as if my whole life was over," she said. "No matter how much you prepare for the possibility of something bad like that happening, you really can't know what it's going to be like until it happens. The grief and numbness that follows. The feeling that nothing will ever be okay again. But in the middle of everything was Mia. This part of Will that was still alive."

She took in a deep breath before continuing. "Then in my third trimester, suddenly I had something else to worry about. The doctor diagnosed me with preeclampsia. I had high blood pressure and my hands and feet were swollen. Once again, I was suddenly facing another crisis."

"You never told me that."

"There was nothing you could do. I didn't even know what to do except follow the doctor's orders. My parents were there for me. I was so scared something would go wrong and I would lose her."

"But you didn't."

"No. And when Mia was finally born, the doctor laid her on my chest and told me she was perfect. I suddenly felt that somehow things would be okay again. Not perfect. Not even happy-ever-after, but okay. It seemed impossible. I was a single mom, about to raise a child on my own, and to be honest, I was terrified and anything but prepared. But this beautiful baby had managed to take away some of the numbness."

"I'm sorry. I wish I could have been there."

"No. I don't want you to feel guilty at all. You came home fighting for your own life. You did exactly what you needed to do." She dropped her gaze. "But I feel like I'm there again. Hearing the doctor telling me the risks of what could happen. I can't lose her, Liam. I can't give them what they want—I don't even know what they think I have—so how are we going to end this? I don't know what to do."

"We're going to find her, but in order to do that we've got to keep going. We need to get to that cabin and get ahold of Griffin. Can you do that?"

She pulled away from him and nodded. "Yeah."

Because Mia was out there somewhere. There was no way she was going to give up.

They started walking again, pressing through the early morning glow of dawn toward the cabin. Snow was falling, but not hard enough that it was slowing them down. Even though Gabby was managing to keep up, Liam was worried about her. She'd proven to be strong over the past few days, but that fall had knocked the wind out of her—and possibly more. He'd continue to monitor her symptoms, but the reality was she needed to be checked out by a doctor, not trooping through the woods in the middle of the night.

He glanced at her silhouette in the soft light. He'd never really noticed how beautiful she was. Those big brown eyes, long hair and full lips… It shouldn't make him feel the way he did, but he couldn't deny it. This was more than just wanting to keep her safe. More than just wanting to ensure they found Mia.

He was falling for her.

Which seemed insane when he stopped and really thought about it. For one, she'd never fall for someone like him. She knew far too well the cost of being a military wife. How could he ask that of her when she'd already lost so much? Expect her to wait for him while he was deployed, never knowing if he'd come home. To deal with him leaving in the middle of the night for a mission he couldn't tell her about. To handle being separated for months on end...

It all sounded so brave and patriotic and even romantic, but what about the day-to-day realities of her having to be a single mom when he was gone. Assuming he was finally cleared for active duty, that was what he had to offer her and that was asking too much.

No, he couldn't—wouldn't—ask that of her.

He could see her breath forming a mist in the early morning air. The sun would rise above the horizon before long, hopefully warming up the temperatures, but they had to keep moving. Their best bet was to find a way to communicate and give Griffin a heads-up as to where the men were likely to emerge on the other side of the forest.

He forced his mind to shift gears and picked up their conversation from the day before. "We started talking yesterday about your struggling to pray."

She hesitated before responding. "Since Will's death, I haven't been able to pray. I mean, really pray. Even if it just meant crying out to God in anger and fear and hope, believing He's really there."

"I think I understand. After the accident, I struggled with so much guilt. I'd watched my best friend die and couldn't stop it. For a while, I took it out as anger against God. Which really didn't make sense, but I didn't know how to cope with what I was feeling."

"What changed things for you?"

"I finally realized that there was something left in the middle of all the loss. That my faith was still there. Not intact, maybe, but there."

"And now?"

"I still struggle to accept what's happened, but I realize that God is there through the healing and doubts now, just like he'll be there in the midst of whatever the future brings. I'm not sure if my doctor is going to approve me for active duty. And without that, I'll end up with a medical discharge and back in civilian life. I'm not sure how I'll deal with that."

"So you don't want to leave the military?"

"It's what I know. Who I am. I honestly can't imagine doing anything else."

He spoke the words, knowing what they would mean to her. Knowing that his need to serve his country meant he could never win her heart.

"You warm enough?" he asked.

"Walking actually helps. Plus, I'm trying to imagine sitting in your house, watching a movie with a huge mug of hot chocolate and marshmallows."

"Ha! What kind of movie?"

"Nothing in particular. I'm guessing you like action. Maybe sci-fi."

"Yep, but they're not your favorite."

"No, but I do love a good apocalyptic movie. You know…end of the world meteor shower or devastating virus."

"Really…then we'll have to make it a date." He stopped, wondering how he'd just opened his big mouth again and said something stupid. "I'm sorry. I just meant, you know, I thought we could hang out some. Like we used to."

When Will was alive. Boy, he was getting good at saying the wrong things.

"I'd like that, actually." Her response surprised him. "Though I have to ask you one question, why aren't you married or at the least dating someone? You're smart, good-looking, funny…"

He glanced at her. "And…"

She laughed. "Seriously. You're a catch."

"I don't know. Saying I haven't found the right person sounds like a cliché, but it's true. And being deployed didn't help, either. Most women aren't looking for someone who's going to be gone a good chunk of the time. It tends to make them run the opposite direction toward the stable guy working a regular job who's always home for dinner."

"I suppose being a military wife takes a certain kind of person and some getting used to—on both sides—but if it's the right person, it's worth it."

"I was always amazed at how you and Will managed to balance your marriage with all his field training and deployments. What about you? Have you thought about dating again, or is it too soon?"

The pause left him regretting his question. "I think I'm going to have to apologize again."

"No...you don't. I just... I haven't really had time to think about it. You mentioned how being deployed didn't help a relationship, try throwing in a baby and a full-time job. Between work and taking care of her, I don't exactly have a lot of free time to go out on dates. Falling in love again sounds frivolous between changing diapers and working full-time."

"I can't see why that would be an issue. Mia's adorable. Just like her mom."

"You'd be surprised at how many guys start

flirting until they notice you're carrying a diaper bag. Then they suddenly vanish out of your life. No. Most guys are not interested in a ready-made family. It's not exactly a Cinderella story."

His hand brushed against her arm as they maneuvered over a spot of uneven ground, making him pause. Why did she look completely kissable? A narrow sunbeam lit up her dark hair. He stopped walking then reached down and pushed back a loose strand from her face, fighting the unwanted feelings of longing that continued to surface. If he kissed her, everything would change. If he didn't, he'd never know what might have happened between them.

And maybe that was best. He was risking far too much by letting this scenario between them play out.

"You look so serious," she said. "What is it?"

"I'm not sure. Maybe it's just the sunrise and this golden halo over you from the sunlight. You're so beautiful."

"I've been out half the night in freezing temperatures, was thrown off a horse and—"

"Trust me." He smiled at her. "You still look beautiful."

"Liam…"

He tried to read her expression, but he couldn't.

"Liam…" She was staring at something behind him. "There's a mountain lion."

EIGHT

Gabby stared at the cat as Liam turned around to face it beside her. Its ears were perked up, head cocked and its gaze aimed right at them like a dart.

"Two rules." He grabbed her arm. "Don't panic. And don't run."

She wanted to laugh at the advice. Running wasn't an issue. She was pretty sure fear had her paralyzed. But panic. Oh, she was already there.

He held up his rifle and started shouting at the cat while waving his hands over his head. She followed his lead, trying to convince the cat—she assumed—that they weren't prey and definitely not this morning's breakfast.

It didn't move. Just stared at them, muscles tense and ready to pounce at any second.

"What do we do?" she asked.

"Keep yelling and slowly move backward."

She waved her arms and shouted at it, staying even with Liam as they took one step back and then another.

Seconds later, it crouched down farther, moving in slow motion as if it were ready at any moment to strike. Her heart raced. She'd heard stories about mountain lion attacks. How they were rare, but still happened. And she wasn't sure which was more terrifying: the men tracking them with their weapons, or the mountain lion less than twenty yards in front of them. She grabbed for the remainders of faith she still held on to.

I'm so tired, God. I've got nothing more to give. I'm going to have to trust You to take over, because I can't stand up emotionally on my own anymore.

The cat kept staring at them. Thirty seconds later, it suddenly stalked off into the bush.

Gabby let out the lungful of air she'd been holding, her eyes still fixed on the spot where it had disappeared. Her heart wouldn't stop racing and adrenaline overload had her exhausted.

"You okay?" Liam asked.

She glanced at the spot where the cat had been, wondering if it was safe to keep moving or if it would return. "I don't know. My heart's pounding."

"Still, I'm impressed. For being normally so soft-spoken, your yell packs a lot of punch."

Her laugh helped deflate some of the stress that had built up inside her, but it only managed to barely soften the edges of this nightmare.

"The good thing is that they don't want an encounter any more than we do," he said. "You just have to convince them you'd make a terrible meal."

"Have you ever been that close to one?"

"Only once. Griffin and I were out hiking. I was thirteen, maybe fourteen. As soon as it disappeared into the bushes, I ran like lightning all the way home. I had nightmares after that for weeks."

She glanced at him. An up close encounter with the animal wasn't the only reason her heart was racing. He was looking at her again with that smile of his, making her realize she hadn't just imagined whatever was going on between them. It was a look that had somehow managed to break through the walls of her heart and leave her defenseless. What in the world had she been thinking, talking to him about dating? Then he'd wanted to kiss her—she was certain of it—catching her totally off guard. What would have happened if she hadn't spotted the mountain lion?

What would have happened if he'd kissed her?

"You think he'll come back?" she asked.

"I doubt it. Like I said, they don't want an encounter with us any more than we want one with them."

She tore her gaze away from him, because whatever she had felt didn't matter. That was a place she couldn't go. She forced herself to refocus. She wasn't ready to put her heart on the line. Not with Liam, and certainly not with another soldier. Not with anyone. It simply wasn't a place her heart could go, especially now of all times.

"How far are we from the cabin?"

He glanced up the trail. "Another mile at the most."

He pulled out his radio and tried to call again.

"Still no signal?"

"Nothing. But it won't be long now."

Despite the sun now hugging the horizon, the temperatures seemed to be dropping and snow was falling again. The wind had picked up and if it kept snowing, it was going to be even harder to maneuver over the terrain. But what choice did they have? With only two ways out, the cabin was closer than going back to the house.

She worked to push away the fear. Fear that Mia wouldn't survive the cold. Fear that her daughter was hungry and wet.

Fear that she wouldn't see her baby again.

Liam wrapped an arm around her as if he understood the emotions flooding through her, leaving her tingling from his touch. "Let's get to the cabin and rethink our plan."

She nodded, then started walking beside him, focusing on the stunning sunrise and her determination to find her daughter instead of his nearness.

You know I'm so tired of doing this alone, God. So tired of feeling like all I'm doing is surviving.

But that didn't mean Liam was the answer.

Or had He answered her prayers before she even asked? She pushed back at the question, wanting to suddenly run away from everything, to beg God to let her wake up back at the ranch in the bedroom with sweet Mia still sleeping in her crib and make all of this go away.

Just because Liam had always been someone she admired, didn't mean she was falling for him. Like Will, he'd volunteered to serve his country, risked his life so she and others could have freedom. She'd never make him leave that for her. But neither was she willing to go back to that life. Falling for him meant a future of deployments, moving and dangers. She knew the toll military life could take on a marriage. Leaving friends and family, giving certain life decisions over to the army, parenting alone, being apart…

She didn't want that again. If God was going to ever send her someone else to love, it would have to be someone who had a normal nine-to-five job.

A flash of color caught her eye about twenty yards to the left. She blinked twice then looked again. She was tired and had to be imagining things, but it was still there. A flash of bright orange in an otherwise gray and white terrain.

"Liam…"

"What is it?"

"I'm not sure, but it looks like Mia's giraffe."

She pulled away from him. She was so tired and cold. Maybe her eyes had simply been playing tricks with her.

A lake spanned out in front of them to the right. The sun shone down on its shiny surface, and it was surrounded by rows of tall spindly trees.

"Gabby, wait… Don't get too close to the edge. The water's frozen, but this time of year it can crack easily."

"I'm not going far. I just need to find out what's out there."

She pulled away from him and walked toward the edge, careful to stay on the ground and not too close to the water. She was a few feet away now. Panic settled in again. It was Mia's giraffe. There was no doubt about it now. But why had they come here? This far off the main trail? Had they known, like Liam, that this was a shortcut to the cabin? She listened for her daughter's cry in the wind. She had to be out here somewhere nearby.

She studied the horizon, looking for a flash of red from the blanket that had gone missing along with Mia.

She turned back to the stuffed animal. It was close now. Only a couple feet away. As she reached out and grabbed the orange giraffe, the ice split beneath her with a loud crack. She hadn't even known she was on the water, but by then it was too late. She heard another crack, screamed, then slid into the icy water.

"Gabby…"

Liam pulled her out onto the solid ground, away from the ice, thankful she hadn't completely fallen through, but even with the sun out, the temperatures were dropping and this was only going to make things worse.

Her lips had paled, and she was shaking. No. This couldn't be happening. Why hadn't he convinced her to stay back at the ranch? Why did she have to be so stubborn? But he couldn't think about that now. He needed to get her to the cabin. He managed to peel off her wet coat, then slipped his on her before shoving Mia's stuffed giraffe into his pocket.

He glanced back at the trail. Thankfully, they were close to the cabin now. Gus would have a fire going and something hot for her to drink. He managed to lift her over his shoulders and started walking. He'd known Gus since he was a little boy. He wasn't sure if the old man would have a cell phone, but he did remember Gus had a ham radio for emergencies.

His limbs felt frozen from the cold by the time he pounded on the cabin's wooden front door.

"Gus... Gus are you in there?"

The door swung open and Liam was met with the barrel of a shotgun. "Put your hands in the air where I can see them now."

Liam's gaze shifted to Gus's bearded face. "It's me. Liam."

"Liam?" Seconds later, the door swung all the way open, and Gus dropped his gun to his side. "What in the world happened?"

Liam didn't wait for an invitation. Instead, he strode into the one-room cabin with a bedroom loft and set Gabby on the thick shaggy rug in front of the fire place. "Sorry to barge in, but I need to warm her up."

"What are you doing out in this weather?"

"Long story, but the bottom line is that she fell in the lake."

"I'll grab something to help warm her up, then get the kettle going. You'll need to take off anything that's wet."

Liam took the pile of blankets Gus handed him, then hurried to get her dry. "Gabby...can you hear me? I need you to talk to me."

"It's so cold." Her teeth were chattering, but at least she was conscious. "And I'm so sleepy."

"I know, and I'm going to warm you up, but I want you to stay awake for now, okay?"

"Where's Mia's giraffe? It was there near the water. She has to be nearby."

"I have the giraffe and we're going to find Mia, but right now, I need to get you warm."

Gus rummaged around in the small kitchen on the other side of the room while the hot water heated up on his stove. "Does this have anything to do with the men that just burst into my cabin about half an hour ago?"

Liam glanced around the room. Nothing looked out of place and Gus seemed fine. At least they hadn't hurt him. "I need to hear exactly what happened as soon as I get her warmed up, but more than likely, yes. Was there a baby with them?"

"Yes. She looked fine. Snuggled up in a

thick blanket, sound asleep. I gave them what they wanted, and they left."

"What did they want?"

"A radio, for starters, but with this storm, communication's pretty impossible. They were trying to get ahold of someone. Ended up taking some water and food and leaving after they'd warmed up."

A minute later, Gus handed him a steamy mug of tea.

Liam helped Gabby sit up, hoping to get as much of the hot drink into her body as possible. "I need you to take a few sips of this."

She pressed her hands against the mug, her fingers still shaking, but at least she swallowed some.

"Good girl." He set the mug on the mantel when she was done, then felt her pulse. It was already stronger than it had been twenty minutes ago. And her breathing seemed more even as well. This could have ended so differently. She'd be okay. He only wished he could say the same for Mia.

There's got to be a way to find her, God. Gabby's already lost so much. Please...please help me find these men.

"Who is she?"

Gus's question pulled him away from his prayer. Gabby had laid her head down on the stack of pillows, her cheeks now flushed from the warmth and her eyes closed again. He stood up and walked across the room.

"Her name's Gabby Kensington. The men that came here have her daughter. I need to get ahold of my brother in Timber Falls and let him know where they are."

"That's actually what I've been trying to do." Gus headed for the desk in the corner of the room. "I didn't mention to the men that I've been tinkering with a new system that allows me to get on to the internet when wireless carrier signals are spotty. Even with the storm, I think I should be able to get through with my antenna. Keep an eye on her and get her to drink the rest of that tea when she wakes up. I'll keep working on getting a message to your brother."

"I also need your ATV," Liam said.

"Sorry, but they decided to split up. One of them took off in it with the baby while the other one left with the horses. They didn't talk much, but from what I gathered, they were heading for Mountain Springs and trying to get ahold of someone." Gus nodded toward the fireplace. "How do you know her?"

"She was married to my best friend, Will Kensington."

"The soldier who was killed back in the Sandbox?"

"Yes."

"I remember you talking about him. And telling me about his death."

"Liam?"

He turned back to the fireplace where Gabby was stirring again. "Hey…can you drink some more tea?"

She managed another couple sips before pushing the drink away.

"Do you feel any warmer?"

She nodded. "I think so, but what about Mia?"

"Gus is trying to contact Griffin right now. We think they're headed to Mountain Springs, which is really the only way out of here. The only easy way, anyway." He brushed back a strand of her hair, knowing he had to tell her everything. "Gus saw Mia."

"What?" She struggled to sit up.

He rested his hand against her shoulder. "Stay still. They stopped here, then one of them took her on his four-wheeler."

"She was okay?"

He nodded. "I don't think they want to hurt her. They just want leverage."

"But I don't have what they want." She pulled up the blanket against her cheek, her eyes welling with tears. "I've got to get up. We need to find her."

"We will, but there's nothing you can do right now. Go back to sleep. Gus will get ahold of Griffin and let him know what's going on, then once the storm passes we can rethink our plan."

She snuggled back down beneath the blankets and closed her eyes, seemingly too tired to argue with him. He watched her breathe. Her heart rate and breathing were regular, and her lips were back to a normal color. But the incident had scared him. For the past year and a half, he'd done his duty checking on her. But he'd also done his best to keep his distance, because he'd carried guilt over not saving Will.

How had all of that suddenly changed? The sense of duty had vanished along with any motivation because of guilt. Now, she'd somehow managed to leave his heart in a tangled mess. He watched her sleep. She looked so calm and peaceful.

The heaviness of fatigue surrounded him as well. All the worry had drained him and he couldn't keep his eyes open. The fire crackled next to him. Gabby's breathing stayed steady as her core temperature continued to rise. But he needed to stay awake. Needed to keep checking on her. As soon as the weather cleared up, he was going to leave her here and go after Mia. But for now, he was so tired.

Movement beside him jolted him awake.

Liam sat up with a start. "I'm sorry. I must have fallen asleep."

The old man dropped another log on the fire. "If you ask me, that's exactly what you needed. Besides that, there isn't much you can do. Snow's coming down pretty hard. It would be foolish to go out there right now."

"What about Griffin? Did you reach him?"

"The connection was bad, but I finally managed to get him a message. The authorities will be waiting for them."

"I need to go out there. I promised Gabby I'd find her daughter."

"I know this isn't easy, but going out into the storm will just put your life in danger. Wait until things clear up some." Gus glanced at Gabby. "That girl there, she's beautiful."

Liam chuckled. "Might be a bit young for you."

"I wasn't talking about for myself. I saw the way you look at her. Looks like you've lost your heart."

He frowned. Surely, how he felt wasn't that obvious.

"I'm just worried about her. But as friends. Nothing more."

"If you say so."

He had to, because falling for Gabby was too

complicated. She'd never give her heart to another soldier, and he couldn't blame her. "She was married to my best friend. It wouldn't be fair to ask her to risk her heart again."

"So you do feel something toward her, you're just too stubborn to admit it."

"Gus…"

"I guess we all have secrets. Pieces of our past we'd like to forget." He hesitated, then pulled out a photo from the desk drawer. "This is my wife and daughter up at Garden of the Gods. We used to hike that loop every summer, even before Kelly could walk. I'd strap on one of those backpack contraptions, so I could carry her. We hiked all the trails. Up to Emerald Lake, the Fern Lake trailhead…"

Liam studied the photo of the three of them. "I never knew you were married."

"I don't tell most people about them. Always ends up making the other person uncomfortable and me…well…it's always easier not to remember. Easier for people to think I'm just a cranky old man who lives in a cabin by himself."

Liam handed him back the photo. "Can I ask what happened?"

"They died in a car wreck on seventy. That was thirty-five years ago."

"You never remarried?" Liam asked.

"Thought about it once. I guess you were right about one thing. Sometimes it's not easy to risk your heart again."

"Do you regret it?"

"I did for a while, but now I can't imagine anyone putting up with me."

"I wouldn't go that far."

Gus caught his gaze. "Just don't do anything you're going to regret one day. Or in your case, don't avoid taking a chance you maybe should take. Love doesn't come around too often, but when it does, you've got to grab onto it and hold on tight."

Liam shook his head. "Now you're starting to sound like my mother. She's always talking about her need for daughters-in-law and grandchildren."

"That's the way the good Lord made us. We love and raise them, then have to send them out of the nest into the world. Grandchildren, I suppose, help feed that loss."

Liam stared into the fire. He couldn't imagine what Gus must be thinking about. How he'd never had the chance to watch his daughter grow up. Never held those grandbabies.

"Liam… I've got a call coming through from your brother."

He went to stand by the Gus, praying for good news. "What have you got, Griffin?"

"We found the pair's abandoned car not far from the ranch and managed to trace it back to Silas Maldin."

"And Mia?" Liam asked.

"I'm sorry, but we still have no idea where she is."

NINE

Liam paced the cabin, trying to fight the restlessness, but the walls of the cabin felt as if they were closing in on him. He glanced at the door, then back at Gabby who was still sleeping next to the fire. Doing nothing wasn't exactly his strong point. His beliefs in both justice and loyalty were what had compelled him to join the military in the first place. And now he needed to do something—anything—to put an end to this.

Like he'd felt ever since the accident.

His jaw tensed at the reminder. Being taken off active duty had sent him to a place he never thought he'd be.

Will was dead, and he'd spent months recovering instead of fighting. Letting someone else wage the war while he was down had left him feeling useless, something he still fought on a daily basis. And according to the army, there were still no guarantees he was going back in.

He turned back to Gus. "I need to do something. I need to be tracking Thatcher down. He's out there somewhere and has to have Mia."

"That would be foolish. Your brother and the police are going to find her. Let them do their job. You need to wait out this storm and make sure Gabby's okay."

Liam glanced over at her again. Her cheeks were flushed, but at least her breathing was still regular. "And if she's not, or if they don't find Mia?"

"She'll be fine. She's strong." Gus stood up from his chair and stretched his back. "Listen, I just checked the weather. There's a break in the storm coming. Temperatures are going to rise a few degrees and hopefully make it easier to navigate the trails. But until then, you need to stay here."

"I know. I just…"

I need to stop this.

For a split second, he was there again. Moments after the IED went off. Moments before his best friend died. He shoved away the memories. The days and weeks after he was transported back to the US. Two surgeries to remove shrapnel and weeks of physical therapy to rehabilitate his leg. On top of all of that was the realization of how much had been lost that day. The guilt that he hadn't been able to stop it.

"You lost a lot over there," Gus said.

"You were in the military, weren't you?" Liam asked, needing to release his emotions.

"Eight years, including two deployments. It changed me. Both for better and worse."

"I keep thinking about what you said. Wondering if Gabby's someone I could see myself with one day."

"Only you can know that, but there's something about the way you look at her. That intense feeling I see in you to protect her. Maybe it's just who you are. Or maybe it's something more."

"It—the thought of us—seems so complicated."

"Why?"

"I'm not sure she'll want to follow me back into military life. She is strong, but that life can be hard. She's already paid the price and knows all too well what can happen. Is it fair to start something with her? To ask her to put her heart on the line again?"

"Have you thought about asking her how she feels? Maybe it's not as complicated as you think."

Liam let out a sharp sigh. "Why is it that love sometimes seems scarier than facing the enemy?" He turned back to Gus. "And I'm not sure I could even consider having a relationship with Gabby. I need someone willing to wait for me when I'm deployed. Someone willing to put up with months of being apart, and the risk of what can happen… It's too much to ask of her."

"Love has a way of making the sacrifices worth it."

But could he start something he wasn't sure she'd be able to finish in the end?

"Liam?"

He moved across the room at the sound of her voice. "Gabby… I'm right here."

He knelt down beside her and brushed a strand of hair out of her eyes. "Hey… I've been worried about you. How are you feeling?"

"It's so cold in here."

He took her hands that had been wrapped beneath the blanket. She was warmer, but there was still a chill to her touch.

I need her to be okay, God. Please. And Mia…

Why did all of this have to happen? He knew no matter what the outcome, things were never going to be the same for him again.

He reached for the tea Gus had heated, which was sitting on the table beside her. "You need to drink more of this. It will warm you. Can you try?"

She shook her head and started to rise. "I can't… I shouldn't be sleeping. We have to get back out there and find Mia."

"Hold on." He rested his hands on her shoulders and laid her back down onto the pillow. "I know how you feel, but we can't go anywhere. Not yet. You're still warming up and there's a storm."

He could hear the panic in her voice. "My baby's out there. I have to find her."

"Gabby, listen to me. The snow has picked up outside. There's supposed to be a break in the weather soon, but right now we can't go anywhere."

"But if she's out there—"

"They would have found shelter for her and them. They need her alive. I've spoken to Griffin. We know where they're headed and the police are mobilized. Griffin is going to let us know as soon as they find her, but they believe she's in town. And Gus saw her, remember? She's okay."

Gabby pulled the ransom note out of her pocket. The ink had run when she'd fallen into the water.

"She has to be close. They were here. We found her giraffe—"

"Why don't you let me make you an omelet," Gus said, interrupting their conversation. "I might not be the best cook on this side of the Rockies, but I went to town a couple days ago and have plenty of fresh eggs. You both need to eat."

Gabby shook her head. "I don't think I can."

"I know this is hard. Waiting always is, but Gus is right. You'll feel better if you eat something."

She nodded, then held out her hands in front of the fire. "I'll try. Is my jacket dry yet? I feel like I'm finally warming up, but I'm still cold."

He grabbed the jacket off the back of the chair to see if it had dried, then shook it out. Something clanged onto the floor. He reached down and picked up a tiny circuit.

"What's wrong?" she asked.

"We might have another problem."

Gabby moved to the hearth to get closer to the fire, not sure she'd ever warm up. "What's wrong?"

"You remember the tracking device they found on your car? The one that enabled them to follow you?"

Gabby nodded, trying not to let fear continue to work its way through her.

He sat down next to her. "I just found another one on your jacket."

"Wait a minute... They're still tracking me?" She ran her finger across the tiny black device. "How's that even possible?"

"I don't know."

Her brain tried to reach through the fog and pull together what had happened. They'd come back to the ranch and this was how they'd found her. How they'd been able to take Mia.

"This gave them the chance to follow me right back to the ranch." Tears welled in her eyes. "They were able to know exactly where I was staying. All they had to do was watch and wait for an opportunity to take her."

But how had they managed to get the tracker in her jacket?

She stared at the chip in her palm. There was only one thing that made sense. "It had to happen at the house. At Casada's. What if they were there to search his house and leave the tracker on his car, or maybe even on his person, but when Casada was killed and we showed up, they took the opportunity to track me instead."

"Giving them a way to follow us and take Mia." Liam stood back up. "That makes sense. If it had been on you before, then they'd already have come out to the ranch. And since they couldn't track you any longer with your car or phone, this was their chance."

The heat from the fire baked her back, but she barely felt it. Instead, guilt swept through her. Guilt that she hadn't been able to keep her daughter safe. That had been her responsibility.

"Gabby." He knelt down in front of her. "This wasn't your fault."

"It doesn't really even matter whose fault it was. I chose to ask questions about Will's death, and in turn put my daughter's life at risk. And now…"

"This isn't your fault," he repeated.

"I hate to interrupt, but he's right," Gus spoke up from the kitchen where he was chopping vegetables for the omelet. "I learned a long time ago that blaming yourself for something you have no control over does little to change the circumstances. And it certainly isn't going to change anything now. What we have to do is find a way to get your daughter back and put an end to this."

"But how?" she asked.

Gus set his knife down and crossed the room. "Can I see it?"

Liam handed the chip to him.

"I used to work with electronics back when I was in the military. Granted, technology has changed over the past few decades, but a lot of the concepts are the same." He pulled out a small magnifying glass from his desk, then sat down in front of it.

"Can you disable it for starters?" Liam asked.

"I should be able to turn it off."

"Will that matter?" Gabby asked. "They have to know where we are by now."

"True, but at least if we leave, they won't be able to track us."

Gus held up the tracker in his palm. "Problem solved. I've disabled it, but I still wouldn't advise going back out there at this point. The snow's yet to let up."

"So we're supposed to just stay here?" Gabby asked.

"I've been battling the same thing," Liam said. "But their options are limited as well. They'd be foolish to be out there in this weather. We're held up inside because of the storm, and I have no doubt so are they."

With Mia.

"Let's focus on what we can do," Liam said.

"Which is?" Gabby asked.

"Try to figure out the end game. What do they want?"

"Evidence of corruption." Gabby said. "Will was gathering evidence of a contractor who was defrauding the government."

"Why didn't Will go to one of his superiors?" Gus asked, now back in the kitchen working on breakfast.

She shook her head. "I don't know, except that he didn't know who to trust."

"You said you spoke to several of Will's superiors," Liam said.

"I did, and no one knew what I was talking about. Unless one of them was lying."

"But that Will wasn't sure who to go to seems significant."

She moved off the hearth away from the fire and back onto the stack of blankets, then pulled one around her. "What do you mean?"

"Will was afraid that it wasn't just the contractors involved, but someone in the military."

"That makes sense," Gus said.

Gabby ran through the implications of their assessment. It did make sense. Why else wouldn't Will have gone to someone? Only if he didn't know who to trust.

"So where do we go from here?" she asked.

Liam headed back to the desk. "Gus, you said your setup here has internet connection?"

"The storm might slow it down, but it should work. I've got a pretty powerful antenna and I was able to contact Griffin once already."

"I want to get an update from him, see if he's

gotten his hands on those military records for Kyle Thatcher."

A minute later, Griffin's voice came over the line.

"Griffin…this is Liam. We're hoping for an update."

"I've been holding off calling you until we had something substantive."

"And Mia?"

"We're still looking. For her as well as Thatcher and Maldin."

"What about Thatcher's army records?"

"They were just sent over, but his file's pretty thin. Looks like he was discharged, then managed to get hired by a contractor and worked for them about two years. I can send you what I have, but it's not much."

"Anyone he stayed in contact with since leaving the military?" Liam asked.

"There's no way to know. Listen, as soon as this weather clears, we'll send an ATV to pick you up. In the meantime, I can send you the parts of his file that are unclassified, so you can see if you can make a connection to something Will said in his letters. We need to find these men. And Gabby, if you can hear this, we've got the entire county looking for your daughter. We're going to find her."

As soon as the file downloaded, she started scanning through the notes, looking for anything that connected with Will's letters.

"Falcon Enterprises… Wait a minute." She turned to Liam. "Do you have your notes on Will's letters on your phone?"

Liam grabbed his phone. "Yes."

"I remember him saying something about a falcon."

"So do I," he said, pulling up his notes.

"At the time, it didn't make sense, but now…" She turned to Gus. "Can you look something up on the internet?"

Gus set one of the omelets in front of her. "As you can see with that file, it's slow, but I can try."

She took a bite of the eggs, surprised at how hungry she was.

"Okay…" Gus said a couple minutes later. "Looks like the company is involved in facilities management for the military. That would include catering, cleaning, laundry, wastes, etc. The company was run by a… Daniel Graham."

"Was?" Liam asked.

"Says Graham was CEO of the company up until about eighteen months ago."

"Right before Will died," Gabby said. "Can you find anything about him after that date?"

"I'm Googling his name, but it's strange... I'm not finding anything. It's like he vanished."

"With government funds, I'd guess," Gabby said.

Gus looked up. "I suppose it's possible."

"If he was working with someone inside the military," Gabby said, "this might all be starting to make sense. Graham defrauds the government but has help from someone on the inside. Then at some point, he takes his money and disappears."

"Will discovers what's going on," Liam said, "but doesn't want to confront one of his superiors without having any solid evidence."

"What about whoever was involved inside the military?" Gabby asked.

"Maybe he found a way out," Liam said. "Or maybe he stashed the money and is waiting until he retires. But just when he thinks he's safe—Will's dead and no one else is suspicious—"

"I start asking questions."

"We're making a lot of assumptions," Liam said, "but they do add up."

Gabby pushed her empty plate away. "Could Thatcher and Maldin have done this on their own?"

"Maybe, but what would be their motivation? Will's letters definitely imply that there's someone on the inside."

"And they have to be the one who hired the men."

Liam shrugged, still not looking convinced. "As much as this makes sense, it really is all just conjecture. There still isn't any proof that Graham is involved."

Gabby moved to the window near the front door where she could watch the still falling snow. A wave of fatigue washed over her. She was so tired, but they couldn't stop yet. There was a piece of the puzzle that was missing, but even if they did figure out what was going on, that wouldn't necessarily be enough to find Mia.

All of a sudden, the sound of splitting wood ripped through the cabin as the door slammed open. A rush of cold air sliced into the room. Gabby lunged away but wasn't fast enough as someone grabbed her and pressed a gun to her temple.

TEN

Gabby sucked in a lungful of air as the intruder wrenched her away from the door and slammed it shut, while still pressing his gun against her head. She looked up, heart pounding, and saw the familiar tattoo on the man's neck. Kyle Thatcher. Why had he returned to the cabin?

Liam and Gus's loaded weapons pointed back at him.

"You're outnumbered," Liam said. "Let her go now."

"Forget it. Set your weapons on the table, or I will shoot her. Because I don't have anything to lose at this point."

Liam took a step forward but didn't drop his gun. "What do you want, Thatcher?"

Gabby caught the man's expression and realized he was thrown at the realization that Liam knew his name. But only for a split second.

"Do what I said," Thatcher said. "This is not a negotiation. Do it, or I will shoot her."

Liam glanced at Gus and nodded. "Okay. We're putting our weapons down, but you need to let her go. None of us are going anywhere."

Thatcher pushed her into a chair, then quickly unloaded their weapons, before putting the cartridges inside his coat pocket.

Gabby fought back a wave of fear, along with the tears that threatened to follow. She didn't care about what happened to them. Her only concern at the moment was finding Mia. "Where's my daughter?"

"She's safe. Don't worry about her."

"And I'm supposed to believe you?" She started to stand up, but he aimed his weapon at her.

"I said she's fine. Sit. Down. Now."

"Just tell me where she is." She bit the edge of her lip, determined not to cry.

"I said she's safe. That's all you need to know."

"You were at James Casada's house," Liam said. "And you're the one who fired on us in the woods, I'm guessing. The police know who you are. They know you ran Gabby off the road and killed Casada. They know you're involved in the kidnapping of Mia."

"I didn't mean to kill him, but all of this…

this shouldn't have happened." Thatcher started pacing in front of her. "And Mia... We didn't have a choice."

Nausea swept through Gabby. "You always have a choice."

He turned around and faced her. "None of this would have happened if you would have done what you were told to begin with."

"Give you evidence? I don't have any evidence."

Liam took a step forward. "Who hired you? We know you didn't do this on your own."

"Stop asking so many questions. There's only one thing that matters right now. My partner made it down the mountains before I did, but now the police are swarming the town. I need another way out of here."

"No chance of that. Your partner took my ATV," Gus said. "Where is it?"

"And where is Mia?" Gabby asked.

"Shut up. I'm the one running this now. Not you."

"Then what do you want us to do?" Liam asked.

Thatcher searched the room. "You had to have let the cops know. How did you communicate with them?"

"Last I recall, you also stole my radio while you were here," Gus said.

Thatcher stormed back across the room, grabbed Gabby by the shoulder and jerked her off the chair. She fought back tears, more from fear than pain.

I don't know how to make this end, God. I know I keep coming to You when things go wrong, but things are going very, very wrong right now...

"Tell me now or I will start shooting."

"Fine." Gus moved to the other side of the room. "I have another system I built."

"What can it do?"

Gus's gaze dropped. "Works with IP infrastructures and connects to Wi-Fi."

"Sounds exactly like what I need."

"Who do you want to call?"

"A cell phone."

"It can do that." Gus headed for the desk. "Give me the number, and I'll set things up for you."

Thatcher nodded back at Gabby. "The two of you stay exactly where you are."

Once Gus had managed to connect the call, Thatcher said, "Colonel Peterson...this is Thatcher. Everything's about to blow up in my face, but I'm not going down alone."

Gabby glanced at Liam, wishing she could talk to him. She'd spoken to Colonel Peterson on the phone, looking for answers. But if he was connected to Thatcher, he could be their inside man.

The radio worked on speakers, allowing all of them to hear the conversation.

"Thatcher...what's going on?"

Thatcher frowned, clearly agitated. "I've got the evidence, but it's going to cost you. Two million dollars."

"Who are you with, Thatcher?"

"All you need to know is that I've just upped the stakes. I've got three hostages now. Plus the baby."

"Okay. Listen, I understand you're upset, but you're just making things worse for yourself."

"Say what you like, but you're out of time, and the stakes have just gone up. If you don't do what I say, I will start killing them. And your involvement in all of this will come out because I'm going to tell everyone."

"Thatcher, listen—"

"No. You listen to me. I want the money transferred. Two million into the account I gave you. No games. No excuses. You got me into this mess, and now you're going to get me out of it. Because if you don't get me my money, I will go to the police and tell them everything you've done."

"Thatcher...you know I don't have that kind of money."

"I've been doing my own digging and we both know you're lying. You've got two hours."

Thatcher hung up the call, then slammed the receiver against the floor before crushing it with his boot.

Gus lunged toward him. "What are you doing?"

"Sit down, old man. You think I'm going to let you give the police a heads-up before we leave."

"Tell me what's going on," Liam started moving toward him. "Maybe I can help you."

"I doubt it. Just sit down and shut up."

"Holding us hostage isn't going to help your case," Liam said. "You're in too deep. I can see that. But it doesn't have to get worse."

"As soon as he transfers the money, I'll be able to disappear."

Liam stopped about four feet from their captor. "Do you really think it will be that easy? He said he didn't have the money."

"He's lying. Colonel Peterson can come up with the money. He got in league with some shady contractor. Why do you think he wanted me to come after you? He's terrified someone's going to find out his secret."

"What is his secret?" Gabby asked.

"A few million government dollars in an off-shore account. The kind of secret that would get him court-martialed and sent to prison for a very long time."

Despite the warmth from the fire, a chill shot through her. "He was afraid I had evidence of what he'd done."

"You're finally catching on. Only his plan to scare you into handing over the evidence didn't exactly work."

"That's because I don't think there is any evidence."

Thatcher started pacing the floor. "This was all supposed to be simple. No one was supposed to get hurt. Casada pulled his gun on me and tried to shoot me. I never meant to kill him."

"You broke into his house," Liam said. "Did you really think that was going to end well?"

Thatcher rubbed the back of his neck. "Stop asking so many questions. There's nothing more to say. As soon as he transfers the money, this will all be over."

"You'll still be a wanted man."

"Do you know how ironic this all is?" Gabby stood up, clenching her hands into fists at her sides. "If Colonel Peterson really is involved, he did all of this for nothing because I have no idea what evidence he's looking for. Don't you see? I don't have the evidence, because Will didn't leave me any. But now my husband is dead, Casada is dead… None of this had to happen."

"He didn't know that."

Gabby moved across the room, stopping in front of Thatcher. "Can I ask you a question?"

"What?"

"Did Peterson have my husband killed because he found out what he knew?"

"I'm sorry about your husband. I really am, but I don't have the answer to that."

"So what happens now?" Liam asked.

"I need to get out of here, and you know this terrain better than anyone." Thatcher grabbed his coat. "You two are going to be my ticket out of here."

"Wait a minute." Liam's jaw tensed. "If you hadn't noticed, there's still a storm out there. Leaving the cabin would be foolish."

Thatcher took a step toward him. "You get me out of here safely, and I'll not only make sure nothing happens to your girlfriend here, I'll make sure she gets her daughter back. But if you try anything stupid, let's just say there won't be a happy reunion."

"And where are we supposed to go?" Liam worked to rein in his temper. "I do know this terrain. Know it enough to realize that the weather's not getting any better, and taking the horses—"

"Forget it. I've already made my decision. The horses have their winter shoes. We'll go through the canyon to Canyon Falls. The authorities won't be expecting us to go there."

Liam glanced at Gus. "They won't be expecting that because they know how foolish that would be. The terrain through the canyon is difficult enough during the summertime but now, even without ice, there's already snow in the high places—"

"He's right, Thatcher," Gus said. "That route is too dangerous this time of year. You need to end this. You're only going to make things worse. What if all three of you end up losing your lives?"

Thatcher clearly wasn't convinced. "We'll manage. The snow has stopped, so even in this weather it can't be more than what…an hour, two at the most, to go down the canyon. She and I will ride together bareback." He turned back to Liam. "That will help ensure you don't do anything stupid on our way out. I'll bet you're trained military. I saw how you tracked us back on the trail tonight. If anyone can get us out of here, you can. And whatever the risk… I'm willing to take it. They won't expect me to go there and it will be a lot easier to disappear once I'm off this mountain."

"I still don't think it's worth the risk," Liam said, needing a way to convince him. "You have a good defense. If Colonel Peterson did everything you said he did, then you can work out a deal with the DA—"

"You think I'm stupid?" He glanced out the window. "They only make deals like that on TV. Not in real life. They won't listen to me. My word—a soldier who was dishonorably discharged—against an army colonel? Who do you think will win? I already know how bad things are. If I stay, I'm going to be charged with murder."

"So what will you do if I can get you off this mountain? Leave the country?"

"That's *my* problem. I think two million dollars will get me wherever I want to go. Grab us something to eat and some water, then we're leaving. And make sure you dress warm enough." Thatcher glanced out the window. "It looks like the snow has finally stopped, so I want to leave now while there's a break in the weather."

Liam frowned, frustrated at being out of control. He weighed his limited options. He and Gus could try to take Thatcher down, but the man was clearly desperate, as well as agitated. Anything they attempted could quickly spiral out of control and get one of them seriously injured or shot. And at this point, it wasn't a risk he felt he could take.

But the other alternative meant facing the danger of going out into this weather through the canyon. This time of year, that was a real risk, not just an excuse he'd come up with. He'd seen the dangers firsthand when joining rescue teams sent to search for lost hikers. Storm slabs often formed over weak layers of snow and could turn into avalanches during periods of heavy snow, especially on slopes and gullies... Exactly the kind of terrain they'd be traversing. And if they ended up caught in a terrain trap, the chances of them getting out alive would be slim. He'd lived most of his life in these mountains and even trained with the army in Arctic conditions for nine months. But all of his knowledge only confirmed that they were making a huge mistake.

His biggest concern, though, was for Gabby.

"Let her stay," he said, slipping on his coat. "I give you my word that I'll do everything I can to get you safely to Canyon Falls, but a third person will simply slow the horses down—"

"Forget it. I make the rules, and I say she's coming. It's time to leave. You, old man, need to sit down in that chair." Thatcher pulled a couple zip ties from his coat pocket, then secured Gus to one of the chairs. "Don't get any ideas about playing hero and going for help."

Outside, the snow had stopped falling and the temperature had risen a few degrees, but none of that took away Liam's worry. A minute later, they took off at a slow, steady pace with him in the lead and Gabby and Thatcher behind him. He'd wanted a moment to talk with her alone. A moment to tell her he was going to do everything in his power to get them safely off this mountain. And what he couldn't do, he could only pray that God would help them end this.

The sun was slowly melting the snow that had covered the ground overnight. But that also left the possibility of sink holes and avalanches from above them. Still, Liam couldn't help but notice the beauty around him. White snow dusted the green trees and canyon walls. On any other day, he would have loved to show Gabby this part of the mountains. While dangerous to the unprepared hiker, the canyon that wound its way next to the river was not only secluded but held some of the most stunning views in the county. But they clearly weren't here to sightsee.

While the canyon narrowed significantly at

several places, it would still be wide enough for the horses to get through. But it was the snow and potential ice, even with the warming temperatures, that had him worried. The horses would be able to adapt to the cold weather, but they could also easily fracture a leg. The risks in his mind were simply too great, but for the moment there was nothing he could do but keep moving, and pray they made it to Canyon Falls in one piece.

The sound of falling ice to his right shifted his attention. He pulled on the reins of his horse, then signaled for Thatcher to stop.

"Move back. Now."

Liam turned his horse around on the narrow trail.

"What's going on?"

A second later, a massive amount of snow crashed down the mountainside from above them like a raging river.

"Liam…"

He had to shout above the noise. "Stay where you are and we'll be okay."

He stroked the horse at the tip of its shoulders, working to keep it calm so it wouldn't bolt.

The eerie silence that followed seemed to swallow them. He studied the rise above, but for the moment, it seemed they were safe. Most of the snow had fallen on the other side of the trail, giving them just enough room to pass. He glanced at the familiar landmarks. Another fifteen minutes and they should be out of here.

Liam felt the tension in his neck begin to dissipate as they finally approached the mouth of the canyon. Sunlight streamed into the valley ahead of them, sparkling on the snow covering the open fields. Liam stopped his horse beneath the sheer red-rock cliffs rising up beside him and waited for them to catch up. "What happens now?"

"My phone should work here. I'll check and see if he's deposited the money."

"And my daughter?" Gabby asked. "You said you'd tell me where she is if Liam brought you here, and he did."

"As soon as I verify the money, I will."

"The trail leads to the edge of town. The horses are worn out and are going to need water and something to eat."

"There's no signal yet. We have to get closer to town so I can connect."

A minute later, Liam caught sight of an older man wearing one of the army's cold-weather jackets and walking toward them near the trailhead.

"Colonel Peterson?"

The colonel took a step forward. "Thatcher... I thought I'd find you here."

An uneasy feeling settled over Liam as they approached the man.

ELEVEN

Exhaustion swept through Gabby, heavier than the cold. All she wanted to do was find Mia and go home, but the realization of who was standing in front of them didn't make sense. If he'd been the one to hire Thatcher, showing up seemed foolish.

Thatcher slid down off the horse, leaving her alone on the back of the animal. "How did you find us?"

"I know you better than you think, Thatcher. I trained you, didn't I? My job was to anticipate your next move and always stay one step ahead of you. Mountain Springs was swarming with law enforcement. You're smart. I figured you'd use the canyon to try and escape, which would mean you would have to pass by here, and I was right."

Thatcher's hands shook as he pulled out his weapon and aimed it at the colonel. "That doesn't explain why you are here."

"I heard what happened on the news and called the authorities. Told them I might be able to talk some sense into you. So despite this nasty weather, I decided to make the drive. They said a man is dead and a baby has been kidnapped. I know you're in a lot of trouble. That's why I came. To help you."

Thatcher took a step forward, tension showing in his jaw. "You thought you needed to talk some sense into me? To help me? Who are you? My shrink?"

"Of course not. But I do think I can help."

Thatcher laughed. "You're lying. You're here to make sure I never get a chance to talk to the authorities. But whatever your plan is won't work. I've told these two the truth. They know everything. You might be able to explain why you shot and killed me, but not all of us. You'll never get away with that."

"You're wrong, Thatcher. I don't want to hurt you. And no one else needs to get hurt. That's why I'm here. Why I want you to listen to me."

"Why should I listen to you?"

"When you first enlisted, you had noble reasons for what you were doing. You ended up getting in with the wrong people and followed them. I know it wasn't your fault. Not entirely anyway. I always wished back then that you would have come to me. I might have been able to fix things.

"You want to fix things? Then tell them the truth." Thatcher gripped the gun with two hands. "Tell them that you're the one who got me into this mess, because I'm not going to prison the rest of my life for what happened. This is on you. Not me."

"Thatcher...listen to me. I know you're upset, and I understand. But you need to put the gun down before someone else gets hurt. And we can't let that happen, can we?"

Thatcher pressed his left palm against his temple. "Why do you keep lying? Is that really what you want? It would be a lot easier to explain why you shot me if I was armed."

"Thatcher, you need to listen to him." Liam got off his horse. "We have to put an end to this now. No one else needs to get hurt."

"I've been talking to the authorities," the colonel said. "They're on their way right now. I just thought we could end this peacefully without anyone getting hurt. Without *you* getting hurt, Thatcher. I was worried what would happen if you didn't feel like anyone here was on your side. Afraid you might do something foolish like shoot someone."

Thatcher took a step toward the colonel. "Don't talk to me that way. Like I'm imagining things. All I did was what you told me to do. I did everything you asked. Broke into her house. Put a tracking device on her car…"

"I've tried to help you, Thatcher. Tried to make you listen to reason." The colonel pulled out his own weapon. "Put the gun down, Thatcher. You know everything you did was your choice, not mine. I'm not going to take responsibility for what happened, but I will help you. Just like I've always tried to do. But not this way."

"He's lying."

Thatcher caught Gabby's gaze. She could hear the panic in his voice but had no idea which one of them was telling the truth. And at the moment she didn't care. All she wanted was to find Mia.

"Everything he says is a lie," Thatcher continued. "He is the one who told me to go after you. To find the evidence Will had and make sure no one ever got it. You believe me, don't you?"

"But there is no evidence, is there, Thatcher?" The colonel kept speaking, his words barely above a whisper. "Because none of that is true. You did this on your own. Everyone knows that. You know that. I know that. The cops know that. It's time to stop and get the help you need."

Gabby got down from the horse, tired of the games. Tired of everything. Thatcher's story about the colonel had been completely believable. But the truth was, she didn't care about who was to blame. She just wanted her baby. And one, if not both, of these men knew where she was.

She walked up to Thatcher.

"Gabby, stay back."

She ignored Liam's warning. "I don't care who did what anymore. All I want is my baby. Where is Mia? You know where she is, Thatcher. You promised me she'd be okay if we did what you said. We came with you here."

Thatcher shook his head. "This wasn't supposed to end this way."

"Where is she, Thatcher?"

"Shut up." He pressed his hands against his ears.

"Thatcher…" Colonel Peterson took a step forward. "Tell her where the baby is. This can stop. All of it. We'll make sure you get the help you need when this is over."

"I don't need help." He was shouting now. The veins in his neck pulsed. "I told you to shut up. All of you. Mia was my leverage to get you to pay. My leverage to make sure you did everything you promised. You told me you'd send the money. Where is the money?"

"We can work this out, but first put the gun down, Thatcher. I just want help."

"It's a lie. You never wanted to help. Never intended to give me the money, did you? You only took advantage of me. Because I know you have it. Five-point-three million dollars. I didn't even ask for all of it. Just enough to allow me to disappear. Tell them that. Tell them you had to wait until you retired before you disappeared with the money."

"None of what you are saying is true, Thatcher, and you know it. All I ever wanted to do was help you, but you never wanted me to. And that is why I can't. There is no money. There never was. I'm sorry. This has to end. I can make sure you get the support you need. Why don't you let me?"

"You were never planning to help me. You lied about the money—"

"You're not listening. There is no money. This was all your imagination. Think about it. All your idea."

"No…no…" Thatcher fired his gun, but his shot missed.

The colonel's return shot hit Thatcher in the chest.

Thatcher dropped to the ground next to Gabby, blood spreading on his abdomen.

"No!" Gabby heard her own scream as she

looked down at Thatcher. "Why did you do that? You didn't have to shoot him. He's knows how to find Mia."

Gabby knelt down beside Thatcher. They couldn't lose him. Not now. Not without knowing where her daughter was.

She yanked off her scarf and pressed it to where he'd been shot. This couldn't be happening. She had to find Mia. "Where is she? Tell me where Maldin took my daughter."

"She…she's safe."

"Tell me where they are…please."

He was rambling now. His face had paled. He was losing too much blood. "He took her to…to a hotel. Pass… I'm…sorry."

Gabby checked for a pulse. Panic ripped through her. He couldn't be dead. Not yet. He knew were Mia was and without him… What if they couldn't find Mia and Maldin?

She grabbed Thatcher's hand, trying to get him to talk to her.

Liam knelt down beside her, then squeezed her shoulder. "He's gone, Gabby, but we will still find her."

"He can't be. We don't know where Mia is." She didn't even try to stop the flow of tears this time. Exhaustion mingled with panic overtook her, sending her to a frightening place she didn't want to go. "We don't know where my baby is."

* * *

Liam pulled Gabby away from Thatcher's lifeless body, still trying to process how quickly things had spiraled out of control over the past couple days. And now he had no idea who was telling the truth. But for the moment, it didn't matter. His priority had to be keeping Gabby safe and finding Mia.

Gabby ran toward the colonel, her cheeks flushed as much from anger, he was certain, as from the cold. She pounded her fists against his chest. "You didn't have to shoot him."

"He shot at me. What was I supposed to do?"

"You don't get it. He took my daughter. Knows where she is, but now—"

Liam pulled her back from the man. He understood her anger and believed it was even justified, but there were still too many unanswered questions to make a judgment.

"It's alright," the colonel said. "I understand. I can't even imagine how terrified you must be right now."

Liam took out his phone, praying Griffin would pick up quickly. "Gabby…what did he say?"

"Just that she's at a hotel. Through the pass, I think."

"Where?"

"I don't know. He didn't say."

Not being able to narrow down where he'd taken Mia was going to make the search more challenging, but starting in Mountain Springs seemed like the most logical step. He turned back to the Colonel. For the moment, they needed the man's help, which meant they had no choice but to trust him.

"Colonel Peterson, do you have a vehicle?"

"Yes. I drove here. My car's parked in a lot just around the corner—"

"Call 911 and get someone here. I'm sure the local authorities are going to need to talk to us about what happened, but we need to get to Mountain Springs."

Gabby stood in front of the colonel while Liam waited for Griffin to answer, her hands at her side, the muscles in her jaw tense. "This is your fault. He told us you put him up to this. That you hired him to search my house and scare me in order to get the evidence my husband had against you. And now, not only is Will dead but James Casada and Thatcher as well. And my daughter… I have no idea where she is."

The colonel shook his head. "I know how all of this looks, and I'm so sorry for everything you've had to go through, but I knew Private Thatcher. He struggled to assimilate into military life until he was discharged. Truth is, he never should have joined the military."

"Griffin...where are you?" Liam said, once his brother answered.

"On my way to Canyon Falls. We just got a lead from a Colonel Peterson that Thatcher is there, but I was about to ask you the same question."

"I'm just outside Canyon Falls. Have you found the other suspect?"

"No, but what about you? How did you get there?"

"Thatcher arrived at the cabin and forced me to go with him as his guide through the canyon. Gabby's here as well. But Thatcher..." He paused before continuing. "Thatcher's dead."

"Dead? How did that happen?"

"Colonel Peterson was waiting for us at the end of the canyon and he shot Thatcher. I was here and saw what happened. It was clearly self-defense. Thatcher pulled a gun on him and shot at him first, but..." He hesitated again.

"But what?"

Liam turned away and lowered his voice. "Let's just say I'm not sure the situation is really as black-and-white as it appears. But there's something more important right now. Mia's still out there somewhere and we need to find her. The second man is our only link right now. According to what Thatcher said before he died, we think Mia is in a hotel, probably in Mountain Springs, but we don't know which one."

"That narrows it down a bit, but there are at least two dozen hotels in town. We'll start canvassing them immediately. We've already set up roadblocks for every way out of town. Wherever he is, we will find him. It's just a matter of time."

"But you need to bc careful. I'm worried about what the man might do. He's going to panic if he finds out Thatcher is dead. And if he decides to use Mia as leverage, we could have a hostage situation on our hands or worse."

"What about the local authorities?" Griffin asked.

Sirens blared as three police cars pulled up. The colonel put his weapon on the ground and raised his hands. "They've just arrived, so I'm going to go for now, but Gabby and I will meet you there as soon as we can. You're going to need all the manpower you can get to find her."

"First, let me talk to whoever's in charge at the scene."

"Put your hands in the air…all three of you."

Liam raised his hands above his head. "My brother, Deputy Griffin O'Callaghan with the sheriff's department in Timber Falls is on the phone and would like to talk to you."

One of the officers stepped forward. "Who are you?"

"Captain Liam O'Callaghan, sir, with the US Army. You can check my ID if you need to."

Liam looked at Gabby while they waited for the two men to talk. Officers were already cordoning off the scene, so they could start their investigation.

"Are you okay?" he asked her.

"I just need to find Mia. That's all that matters right now."

He squeezed her fingers. "We're going to find her."

A minute later, the officer walked back to them. "Your brother's pretty convincing. I'm still going to need full statements from both of you, but in the meantime, I'll have my deputy drive you to Mountain Springs so you can help with the search. But you, sir…" He turned to Colonel Peterson. "You're going to have to come with us now so we can get a complete statement."

"Of course. I understand."

"And the horses?" Gabby asked.

"I'll have one of my officers take care of them."

* * *

An hour and a half later, they were canvassing hotels in Mountain Springs with two officers from the local police station. Liam still had a pile of questions, including why the colonel had suddenly appeared and, even more disturbing, had he really felt forced to shoot Thatcher. But only one thing really mattered right now, and that was finding Mia.

"How many hotels are left?" She glanced at him as they pulled into the parking lot of their third hotel.

"This is one of the last ones," Officer Thompson answered.

Her frown deepened. "This is like looking for a needle in the haystack. We don't even have any guarantees that they're still in Mountain Springs. And if Maldin saw the news... knows that Thatcher is dead, his next move is going to be to get as far away from here as possible. What if we're too late?"

He squeezed her hand, feeling her frustration. "She's got to be here. The authorities have set up roadblocks. Wherever this guy is, he's not going anywhere, and he knows it. Someone out there has seen her."

"What do you want us to do?"

"The two of you take this one. We'll take the one across the street."

"And after that?" Gabby asked.

"We're going to find her, Gabby. Whatever it takes."

They climbed out of the squad car and headed for the hotel lobby. Gabby's worry was justified. Pretty soon, they would have to expand the perimeter of the search.

Liam burst into the lobby of the hotel in front of Gabby and stepped up to the receptionist. "Have you seen either of these men? Possibly with a baby."

The clerk stared at the photo a few seconds, then shook her head, clearly not interested in getting involved. "Sorry. I don't think so."

"Please look at this again. This is my baby." Gabby leaned against the counter. "Are you sure?"

The woman glanced back at the photo a few more seconds. "Actually… I think I do recognize him, but I don't want any trouble here."

"He kidnapped the baby he was with," Liam said.

"Kidnapped?" The woman's face paled. "He told me his wife was sick and had just been admitted into the hospital. Made me feel so sorry for him. I can't believe he's wanted by the police."

"What room is he in?" Liam asked.

"He was in room 124."

Gabby rushed out of the lobby in front of Liam toward the row of rooms with parking-lot access while he called in their find to the authorities. He had no desire to confront an armed man on his own, but if he had to, he would.

The door to room 124 swung open as they approached.

"Mia?"

The little girl was sobbing in a crib in the back corner of the room. Maldin tried to shut the door, but Liam stopped it with his foot. Rushing across the room, Maldin dropped the ice bucket he'd been holding, grabbed Mia out of the crib and held up a gun. "Stay back. Both of you. Or I will hurt her."

TWELVE

Gabby caught the desperation in the man's voice. Mia whimpered in his arms. So close and yet she couldn't go to her without risking her daughter's life. Maldin was panicked. She could see it in his eyes. They couldn't count on the police to get here in time, which meant they needed to find a way to stop him before someone got hurt.

She grabbed onto Liam's coat. "We've got to get her out of here," she whispered.

"We will." He grabbed her hand, his focus trained on the man standing in front of them with a gun. "Silas Maldin... That's your name, isn't it?"

"How do you know that?"

"We saw Thatcher up at the cabin."

Sweat beaded on his forehead despite the cold temperatures. "Thatcher told me to wait here, then never showed up."

"Thatcher never should have done that,

but this is over. I want you to give Mia to her mother, because if you hurt her, you're going to be in a lot more trouble and I don't think either of us wants to see that happen. The police are already here and will be at your door any second now."

Mia was crying harder now, her cheeks flushed red as she squirmed in the man's arms. Gabby's fingers pinched Liam's arm.

"Please let me have her. She's hungry and tired."

"I don't want her to get hurt. I don't want anyone to get hurt, but in order for that to happen, you're going to have to do what I say."

"Then tell me what you want," Liam said.

"A way out of here. We never meant to hurt that man. The money they offered us was good, but we never meant to hurt anyone. Instead things got out of control. That man was shot in self-defense."

While you were burglarizing his home.

She bit back the sharp response on the tip of her tongue. Angering him further wasn't the answer, but what was? He wasn't going to take responsibility for what he'd done. In his eyes, he was the victim.

"That might be true, but we don't want that to happen again." Liam's voice was calm and steady. "Not only have you killed a man, you've kidnapped Mia."

"That was only for leverage. We never would have hurt her."

"Then let me help you find a way to put an end to this. I'll help you deal with the police, but give us the baby."

He shook his head. "I can't go back to prison."

"You can make a deal with the DA for a lesser sentence. Who hired you, for starters?"

Shadows breached the window, turning the man's attention to the front of the room.

"Who's out there?" he asked.

"I'm guessing the officers who've been looking for Mia."

"Tell them to get back or someone's going to get hurt."

Liam held up his hands. "I've got their direct number. I'll tell them."

Gabby studied Liam's expression for a moment while he talked with the police, then looked back at Mia. She was so close. A dozen steps away and crying, and yet there was nothing she could do.

We're so close to this being over, God, but I feel so hopeless.

Liam hung up his phone. "The officers are

moving back, but we need to find a way to end this without anyone getting hurt."

Maldin leaned against the yellowed walls, trying to get Mia to stop crying. "Can you make her stop?"

"Just let me take her. Please."

"I can't do that. She's my leverage."

Liam squeezed Gabby's elbow, then took a step forward. "Let's figure a way out of this together. It is correct someone hired you, right?"

"Yes, but Thatcher never told me who. Told me it would make sure I didn't get into trouble if things went wrong. The less I knew the better. But now... I just know that I need to get out of here."

"Here's what I know," Liam said. "If you run, you're only going to make things worse. But if you end this now—give Mia back to her mom and give yourself up—you'll have more of a chance of making a deal. I promise."

"Forget it. One way or the other, I'm going to walk out of here free."

"Where do you want to go?" Liam asked.

"It doesn't matter, but here's my deal. I need unmarked cash. Enough to get me somewhere I can't be traced."

Mia continued to fuss, and Gabby could tell by Maldin's expression that he was getting irritated. Despite Liam's calming voice, she felt her own anxiety growing. Because at this point, was whatever he said going to be enough?

Gabby drew in a deep breath. "She's hungry. There's a vending machine around the corner. Let me get something for her. It will calm her down. Please…"

Liam pulled a dollar out of his pocket and handed it to her. "Let her go get something. I'll stay here with you."

Maldin hesitated, then nodded. "Don't do anything stupid. Get her something and come straight back."

"I will. I promise."

"And don't talk to anyone out there. Because if you do, you won't see either of them again." He glanced at his watch. "You've got ninety seconds starting now."

Gabby slipped out of the room, praying her legs wouldn't give way as she followed the sign and turned down a narrow hallway. Paint was chipping off the walls as if the place hadn't been repaired for years. But she barely saw anything. Griffin and his men were here somewhere, but clearly following the instructions to stay out of the way.

She slid the dollar into the vending machine, then pushed the button for a bag of cheese crackers, feeling the weight of the situation pressing against her chest like a vise. It might not be something she typically bought for Mia, but at least it should calm her down.

She jumped as ice clanked in the machine next to her, dumping a batch of frozen cubes.

Griffin stepped up next to her. "Did he let you go?"

"He gave me ninety seconds to buy something for Mia to eat," she said. "But I have to go back."

"Which gives me about thirty seconds. What's going on in there?"

"He's alone but motivated by fear. He wants out of this but is afraid of going back to prison. He wants cash to drive out of here."

"Where is he standing?"

"Toward the back of the room. He's got a handgun…a Glock…and he's holding Mia."

"Which definitely limits our options. We've got a SWAT team lined up. Try to get him to let you take Mia. Then get him by the window if you can, though with the three of you inside we won't take any unnecessary risks."

She caught Griffin's gaze and realized what he was saying. But as much as she didn't want anyone to get killed—including Maldin—she knew she'd fight to save her daughter.

"As a last resort only, I promise."

She nodded before heading back to the

room, carrying the crackers and her hands held up. Mia was still fussing in Maldin's arms, her eyes red from crying. "Can I take her? Please? It's the only way she'll stop fussing."

He hesitated, then handed her to Gabby. Mia lunged into her arms, then nestled her head on her mom's shoulder still sobbing. "Hey, my sweet girl. How are you doing? Mama missed you so much."

Mia pulled back and looked up at her, big tears running down her cheeks. Gabby opened the cheese crackers and gave her one.

"Sit down over there, because this isn't over." Maldin paced the worn carpet in front of her but away from the window. "I still need a way out of here."

Gabby glanced at Liam. It was clear Maldin had no clear plan and was simply winging it, but she also knew it wasn't going to take much for him to explode.

"Thank you," Liam said. "You made the right decision letting her go back to her mother."

"Maybe, but here's the plan," Maldin said. "I want you to call the police again. Tell them I want ten thousand dollars cash and a car. I'll take the two of them with me to make sure I'm not tailed. If my instructions are followed, I'll leave them somewhere safe. But that means no one comes after us. No cops."

"That can't happen, Maldin." Liam took a step forward. "But I'll make a deal with you."

"What kind of deal?"

"I'll go with you. I'll leave with you and guarantee that no cops follow you. I'll take you somewhere safe where you can disappear."

"There are roadblocks. I saw it on the news."

"I'll get you past them. I'll be your hostage. But let them go."

Gabby tried to swallow the lump that had formed in her throat. "Liam, no—"

He signaled her to be quiet. "I'll go with you, but that means you let Gabby and her daughter go. They don't need to be involved in this any longer."

The man glanced at the window. "No games?"

"No games."

Gabby pulled Mia closer against her chest and sat down on the edge of the bed. There had to be another option. One that didn't involve either of them leaving with the man. Once he got wherever it was he wanted to go, he wouldn't need any of them. It was too big of a risk.

"Liam, you can't go with him."

"I want this over as much as you do. Trust me." He turned back to Maldin. "My brother's a deputy in Timber Falls. I can have him arrange your demands."

"Call him, but put it on speaker phone."

Liam placed the call, then held up his cell. "Griffin... I've made a deal with Maldin. He's going to let Gabby and Mia go, and in exchange, I'm going to drive him out of here. He's also demanding ten grand."

"Ten grand? That will take time to get together."

"You've got thirty minutes," Maldin said. "Pull all cops back at least three blocks and leave the money and something for lunch outside my door. If you follow me or try to do anything, I will kill your brother."

Thirty minutes later, Gabby felt her lungs constrict as she watched Maldin walk Liam out of the hotel room. The man stood behind Liam so there wasn't the possibility of the sniper taking him down from his position. Which meant there was no way out of this for Liam. Everything that had happened over the past couple days pressed in around Gabby. Mia was safe, and for that she was grateful, but this was far from over.

Griffin stepped into the room. "Are you both okay?"

"Yes, but you can't let Liam drive away with that guy. There has to be another way."

"I'm not sure we have a choice. When you're driven by fear, you don't make logical decisions. If we interfere at this point, someone's going to get hurt. And that someone's going to be Liam."

"Yes, but you can't just let him leave. Is there a way to track him?"

"We're counting on it. We'll be able to keep tabs on where they go through the GPS on the car and possibly through their cell phones as well. I've got a tech already working on it. And in the meantime, Liam's trained to handle situations like this. He's going to be okay."

Except he couldn't promise her that.

"And you think that will be enough to ensure Liam's safety?" Mia started fussing again. Gabby handed her another cracker. Liam had traded himself for her and her daughter. She owed him their lives. There had to be something she could do to help.

"Everything we could find about Maldin— which wasn't much—shows that he has a temper and is impulsive. So as much as I hate the call Liam made, there weren't many options. I don't think it would have taken much to set him off."

"But what happens when he's done with

Liam? If he gets to where he thinks he's safe, then Liam is no longer insurance but a liability."

"We're following protocol as much as possible, but things don't always play out the way we want them to. In a sense, Liam has become the negotiator, the setting has just changed. But Liam can handle this. He took the man seriously, showed empathy and gave him an option—"

"An option that could cost Liam his life."

Griffin sat down next to her. "I know this is hard, Gabby, but Liam knew what he was doing, and I can promise you, he doesn't want you to feel guilty for the situation he's in. None of this is your fault."

"None of this would have happened if I hadn't come to him."

"What do you think would have happened if you'd faced those men alone? You did the right thing, because no matter what you think, he feels responsible for you. And that kind of responsibility isn't something Liam takes lightly."

"But what if he's killed?"

"I have no plans of taking any chances with my brother's life. Which is the one reason I let them walk out of here without any physical force involved."

"He saved my daughter, but if anything happens to him… I just need to do something."

"I am going to need your help. I know you're exhausted, but we need to take a full statement on everything that's happened while it's fresh on your mind, then we'll get you and Mia out to the ranch where my parents are waiting. And in the meantime, I promise to keep you updated on what's going on." He stood up and signaled to one of the other officers. "We'll get him back."

She nodded. "I'll do everything I can to help, but what do you think Maldin plans to do?"

"Hopefully, as soon as they're far enough away that Maldin feels it's safe to disappear, he'll let my brother go."

"And if he doesn't?"

Mia started fussing again. Gabby needed to get her to bed. And Mia wasn't the only one exhausted.

"Liam can handle a situation like this, Gabby. He's trained and he's smart."

"I know, it's just…" She pressed her lips together, unable to sort through the pile of emotions fluttering to the surface. She could taste the metallic flavor of blood where she'd bitten her lip. She grabbed Mia's giraffe and gave it to her. Right now, she needed to focus on her daughter, tell the detectives anything that might help put an end to all of this and let the authorities do their job.

But what if that wasn't enough to bring Liam back safely?

"We'll try to keep it short, so you can get her to bed."

"What will you do?"

"Make sure we keep our tail on him, for starters."

"I trust you. I trust Liam, but Maldin…he was involved in Casada's murder and now the stakes are rising. He's staking everything on getting away no matter how foolish his plan is, and he'll do anything to ensure he doesn't go back to prison." She grabbed Mia's blanket, then stood up. "There's something else you need to know. According to Kyle Thatcher, Colonel Peterson is the one who hired them."

Griffin stopped in the doorway. "What?"

"He's the one who hired Thatcher and Maldin. The one who's been behind all of this."

"Thatcher told you that?"

"Yes."

"The colonel told us Thatcher had accused him of a number of things, but so far there is no evidence that points to the fact that Thatcher was working for Peterson. In fact, everything we have so far indicates Thatcher and Maldin were working alone."

Gabby shook her head. "He told us everything in detail. Why would he have made all that up?"

"Clearly, he didn't want to go to jail. I'm not sure what his plan was, but I've seen it dozens of times. People in Thatcher's situation never take the blame for what they did. They always try to transfer it to someone else."

Gabby paused. Hadn't Maldin done the same thing? Pushed the blame for what had happened on to someone else? But Thatcher had been convincing with details and the timeline of what had happened. He knew things that made the colonel's involvement seem plausible.

"But what if he's telling the truth?" she asked.

"We will continue to investigate everything that happened, but so far there just isn't any evidence."

No evidence of his involvement seemed impossible. Unless Colonel Peterson really was telling the truth.

"Gabby, I promise we'll get to the bottom of this. But right now, we need to go. I'm concerned about Liam's safety as much as you are."

"I know. And I'm sorry. He's your brother. I know you care. I just feel as if I owe him so much."

My life. Mia's life...

Mia's head lay burrowed in Gabby's shoulder as she shut her eyes and her breathing deepened. The poor baby was exhausted. They were both exhausted.

"I'm going to drive you back to the ranch," Griffin said. "I can take your statement from there. Just know we're doing everything we can to find him."

"I know."

Ten minutes later, she held back the tears as she put Mia into the car seat. She slid into the back seat next to the little girl and put on her seat belt. She felt numb and scared. Liam had saved her daughter's life. Now they just had to make sure they saved his.

Gabby took Mia's small hand and enclosed it in her own. Liam would be alright. She had to believe that.

She stared out the window, still holding Mia's hand. The snow had stopped after leaving several inches behind. But she barely noticed the view. What if she never saw Liam again? The thought of something happening to him hurt, but it shouldn't hurt this much. It shouldn't feel like her heart was shattering into a thousand pieces. He was just a friend. Someone who'd been close to Will and who had helped her out of obligation. Nothing more.

And certainly not someone who'd managed to wedge his way into the recesses of her heart and made her wonder for the first time if loving someone again was even possible.

Was it?

Will had told her once if he didn't come home from deployment, he wanted her to fall in love again and get remarried. At the time, she'd fiercely rejected the idea and felt it would somehow be unfaithful to her husband. Instead, she'd imagined them growing old together. A houseful of kids. Summer vacations and skiing in the winter. Not losing him like this. But reality was never as nice and neat as a fairytale whcre the bad guys always lost and the prince and princess always lived happily-ever-after.

But what about second chances? What about picking up the messy baggage and trying to put the pieces together for something new? Was that even possible? Maybe. Eventually. But Liam… She couldn't fall for him.

Memories surrounded her. Every time Will had left for deployment or for another mission, she'd carried her phone with her everywhere she went, constantly checking to make sure the ringer volume was up and she hadn't missed a call.

Which was the problem. If she allowed

something to happen with Liam, she'd be right back in the same place again. Liam was a soldier, dedicated to his country. That was who he was. Brave, loyal, heroic… It was what she loved about him, but when it came to her heart…that was another story. That wasn't going to happen again. Couldn't happen again. Because getting involved emotionally would be disastrous for her heart.

THIRTEEN

Liam pushed his way through Denver traffic, heading north as instructed. Maldin had insisted he drive but made it clear if he did anything to get someone's attention, he wouldn't hesitate to make him pay. And with the man's nerves clearly strung tight, Liam had decided to simply follow directions and wait for an opportunity when he could put an end to all of this without the risk of someone getting hurt. Besides, all that really mattered right now was that Gabby and Mia were safe. That had been his goal through all of this. He'd find a way to take the man down, but right now wasn't the time.

He glanced into his rearview mirror at the tan sedan four cars back. He'd spotted the tail when they'd left Mountain Springs and hoped Maldin hadn't noticed. But he couldn't be sure. The guy wasn't stupid.

What he didn't know was if Maldin actually

had a backup plan in place, or if he was simply figuring things out as he went. The man had been on the phone on and off for the past thirty minutes, talking to someone about an apparent exit strategy, but Liam had no idea who he'd gone to for help. But assuming the man had no plan and no resources would be a mistake. He had a loaded gun and if given the right circumstances, there was no doubt in Liam's mind that the man would use it.

Maldin let out a huff of air, then dropped his phone into his lap. "I want you to take the next exit, then turn left at the light."

"I'll try, but the traffic's heavy." Liam turned on his blinker from the center lane, then started to merge into the exiting lane. "Where are we heading?"

"You don't need to worry about that right now."

Maldin glanced into his side window again and frowned. There was no doubt in Liam's mind anymore. The man had discovered the tail.

"Something wrong?"

"Don't be stupid. I told them no tails, and they've got someone behind us." He fingered the gun in his lap. "You will lose them, because I'd hate for your brother to find you dead in some ditch when all of this is over."

Liam took the exit ramp, then quickly made a left turn at the green light. He followed the man's instructions, weaving through the heavy traffic in an attempt to ditch their tail. A mile later, he glanced at his rearview mirror. The tan car was nowhere in sight.

"Keep heading north. We'll turn off in a few minutes."

Liam tightened his fingers around the steering wheel, wishing he were home right now eating dinner with his parents and Gabby. His mother had told him she was planning to make lasagna, one of his favorites. He'd been looking forward to spending time with Gabby. Instead, he didn't want to know what his mother was thinking right now. He knew she worried every time one of her boys found themselves in a dangerous situation, which happened more often than not in their lines of work. Maybe he hadn't told her enough how he felt.

But he knew she would understand his decision. Taking Gabby and Mia's place had been automatic. He'd have done the same for anyone. Or at least that's what he'd tried to convince himself of. He was still sorting through his feelings toward Gabby. Feelings he probably wouldn't be able to fully process until all of this was over. And when it was over, they'd both go their separate ways, but he'd still feel responsible for her. There was no doubt about that. But he also couldn't ignore that there was something more.

Maldin's threats to take Gabby and Mia had shown Liam how terrified he was of losing them. There was nothing really noble or brave about his decision. It was simply how he'd been trained and who he was. And a reminder of how he wanted them in his life.

He glanced over at Maldin as he followed the now narrow road northwest. He wasn't sure building a rapport with the man sitting next to him was possible, but it was worth a try. The more he could understand Maldin's motivation and even possibly figure out what his plan was the better.

"Thank you for letting them go," Liam said.

"Are you the baby's father?"

He glanced at the man, surprised at his question. "No."

"Then why do you care what happens to her?"

"She was my best friend's daughter."

"Something happened to him?"

"He was killed."

His answer was ignored. Gaining Maldin's sympathy wasn't working. The man clearly had no desire to talk with him.

He decided to try a more direct approach. "Where are we heading?"

"Another fifty miles or so. I've got a friend with access to an airstrip. I'll let you go once we're there, as long as you don't try anything in the meantime."

"You know you don't have to follow through with this," he said. "The sooner you turn yourself in, the fewer charges you'll be facing. Being a fugitive isn't easy."

"Turn myself in? Forget it. I don't have anything to lose at this point."

Liam shifted in his seat, frustrated. Because he did.

The thought surprised him. The past year had taken a toll on him emotionally. Months of physical therapy had meant hard work mixed in with occasional bouts of depression. And he still had no idea if he was going to be able to go back to active duty. The decision had been taken completely out of his hands and weighed heavily on him, leaving him feeling out of control. Like he'd lost everything he'd worked for in one moment.

The moment that had killed his best friend.

Except for the occasional command, silence hovered between them until Maldin directed him to turn off down a narrow gravel road lined with trees. The headlights caught a deer running out in front of them in the cover of dusk, pulling Liam back to the present. He slammed on his brakes and skidded on the gravel, barely missing the animal. The car slid to a stop, but his heart kept racing.

"What are you doing?" Maldin braced his hands against the dash. "Trying to get us both killed?"

"Hardly."

Maldin banged on the console between them. "Keep going. We're running out of time."

Time for what, he wasn't sure. He focused his attention back on the road. Darkness began to settle in around them, forcing him to drop his speed. On top of that, he wasn't sure where they were. No other cars. No cabins. Wherever they were going was isolated. There were a handful of private airstrips, and if Maldin had the right connections, it would be the easiest way out of here. Though where the man would go, Liam had no idea.

"We're here. Stop the car, then get out."

Liam checked the odometer, then turned off the car. Maldin snatched the keys out of his hand. They'd driven just over twenty miles from the turnoff. He stepped out of the car. The temperatures were dropping again, and a dusting of snow already covered the ground.

"Where are we going?"

"You're not going anywhere. Get out."

"You're leaving me here? We're twenty miles from the main road."

"What did you expect? I could shoot you, too, but instead I think I'll let you walk out of here. There are no cell phone towers nearby and very little if any traffic. But it's the best I can do."

"So I'm guessing there isn't a cabin or somewhere I can stay till morning?"

"That's not my problem."

The question probably sounded ridiculous. He was a hostage, not a guest. Maldin had made that clear.

Liam shivered as he looked around, wishing he had his heavy coat that had gotten left at the hotel. Unlike his parents' ranch, he didn't know the terrain. While Maldin might have let him go, this wasn't over. If he didn't find shelter, he wouldn't make it through the night.

Gabby sat in the O'Callaghan living room, telling Griffin everything she could remember about the past twelve hours. But relaying the details about Thatcher and their conversation in Gus's cabin and the moments surrounding the man's death felt more as if she were reciting scenes from a movie. Certainly not from her own life. The knot of fear in her gut tightened, reminding her that this was all too real. And until they found Liam, she wasn't going to be able to put all of this behind her.

Griffin's phone rang, giving her a brief respite from steady stream of emotion that had come with the retelling of what had happen. He checked the caller ID, then stood up.

"Give me a sec… I need to take this call."

"Of course."

She glanced down at Mia, who had finally gone to sleep and was now breathing softly in her lap. At least one thing had gone right today. Mia was finally safe.

Griffin walked back into the room a few moments later and stopped in front of her. "We have a problem."

"What's wrong?"

"Apparently Maldin had a jamming device on him, and my team lost visual contact. They have no idea where Liam is."

"Wait a minute…" A rush of adrenalin ripped through her as she stood up. "Isn't there a way to—I don't know—disarm it?"

"There is, but it's not easy. Maldin must have figured out he had a tail and made sure Liam ditched the officers."

Gabby pressed her fingers against her temple. "What happens now? There's got to be an-

other way to track them. A phone…the car…
city surveillance cameras…something."

"There's a statewide search on the vehicle.
He won't be able to get far. But we also have
to ensure that law enforcement doesn't engage
Maldin."

Which meant finding Liam had just gotten
more complicated. Without having any idea
what Maldin's plan was—or even if he had a
plan—they could have potentially gone anywhere. It was about thirteen hours to the Canadian border and less than that to the Mexican
border. Depending on his connections and how
much he was willing to risk, there were also
airstrips and bus terminals scattered across
the state.

But there was one lingering question that
scared Gabby more than anything else. When
Maldin got to wherever he was going and
didn't need Liam anymore…what was going
to happen?

She tried to shake off the growing layer of
fear as she entered the ranch house. Marci
met her and Mia at the door with a big hug,
then ushered them straight to the kitchen that
smelled like garlic and onions. Her stomach
growled, reminding her it had been hours since
she'd eaten. Maybe she was hungry after all.

"I knew you'd find her." Marci squeezed

Mia's hand. "I know you must be so relieved. Griffin's been keeping us updated and we've been praying nonstop."

"I am relieved, but Liam's still out there."

A shadow crossed Marci's face. "They're going to find him. He was trained to handle situations like this. He'll be fine."

Gabby nodded. She knew Liam was trained to handle a crisis, but as relieved as she was to have Mia back, his situation dented her relief. Because this wasn't over. Liam was out there somewhere, and if the colonel was involved—like she was still convinced he was—this was far from over.

What if he came after her again?

"How is she?" Marci asked.

Gabby glanced down at Mia who was awake but nestled quietly against her chest. "They had someone check her out at the station, and she was just a little dehydrated. And clingy."

"I don't blame her." Marci kissed Mia on the forehead. "Can I get you some lasagna? There's plenty."

"I didn't think I was hungry, but it smells wonderful. I think I can eat a small helping."

A minute later, Marci set a plate of the pasta in front of Gabby along with a slice of garlic bread. "If you want to put Mia in the high chair, I can get her something as well."

"Thank you." She set Mia in the high chair, hoping the little girl would be able to stay awake long enough to eat something. "You've done so much for Mia and me. And I'm sorry for dragging your family into this. I know you have to be scared—"

"Don't even go there. Griffin told me you were feeling guilty over what happened. Don't. I know my son well enough to realize that everything he did, he did because that's who he is. And no matter how much I worry about him, I know he'd make the same decision again in a heartbeat. He won't have any regrets, which means I can't, either. What I can do is pray, something I've been doing a lot of lately."

Marci set a few bits of finger food on the tray in front of Mia, then watched her daughter perk up.

"That has to be hard," Gabby said. "Knowing they're all out there willing to take risks that most people would run from."

Marcy caught her gaze. "You know what that's like."

She nodded, then took a bite of her bread.

"I remember the first time Liam told me he was going to be a soldier. He wanted to be just like his grandfather. It was at that point I realized my boy was a warrior. And really, I guess all my boys are warriors in their own way. For justice and duty. I'm proud of them, but that doesn't mean it's been easy. A mom's job is to love and support her children but taking worry out of the mixture feels pretty impossible most days. Today especially."

Gabby set down her spoon and shook her head. "How do you do it then? Get through another day of worrying."

She might not have any claims on Liam or his heart, but that didn't take away her own worry for him.

Marci filled a mug of coffee for herself, then came and sat down next to Gabby. "I've learned that the only thing I can really do is trust them into God's hands. There are no guarantees in life whether they're deployed or working right here in Timber Falls. God created Liam to be a soldier. That's who he is. And in the end, I have to trust God's plan for his life. I don't always succeed, but I try to shove the worry aside and concentrate on the moments I have with him. It's the only way I've found to get through life. For now, they're out there looking for him and I have to believe they'll find him. My advice for you right now would be to finish eating, then get some sleep. And I'm praying that all of this will be over by morning."

Gabby set her fork down. "Thank you."

"Did you get enough to eat?"

"I did. Thank you."

"Why don't you go upstairs and take a shower before you go to sleep? I'll get Mia cleaned up and watch her for you."

Gabby glanced at Mia, whose eyes were starting to close. But she still hesitated, unsure if she was ready to leave her daughter, even for a short time.

"She'll be fine," Marci said. "Poor girl's exhausted, and I know you are, too. I'll go rock her in the living room, then you can both get some sleep."

Twenty minutes later, she was thankful she'd washed off the grime from the past day.

She'd just slipped into a fresh pair of flannel pajamas Marci had left for her and now went to find Mia already asleep. She took the sleeping girl from Marci and nestled the child against her shoulder.

"Will you promise me one thing?" Gabby asked Marci.

"Of course."

"If there's an update on Liam… I don't care what time it is…will you let me know?"

"You bet. And Gabby…" Marci hesitated in the doorway. "I'm probably completely overstepping my bounds for saying this, but I've waited a long time for my boys to find themselves good wives. Sometimes I wonder if I'll actually live to see the day I have grandchildren." She let out a low laugh. "I just hope Liam finds someone like you one day."

A moment later, Gabby closed the door behind her, then carefully laid Mia in the crib next to her bed. She didn't want to read into Marci's words. The woman hadn't said that she wanted Liam to marry her specifically, but the implication had been there.

None of that mattered. Not tonight.

She moved to the window, pulled back the heavy curtains, then checked the lock. It had started snowing again, and moonlight reflected off the white ground. Liam had saved her and Mia because that was who he was. A hero, in her eyes. One who'd chosen to take her place in the face of danger. Which was why she needed to compartmentalize what her heart was feeling. His actions didn't speak to his feelings toward her, but to something greater. His sense of duty and honor. But for some reason, she was having a hard time separating the two. Tonight, though, had proven once again why she couldn't fall for him. His willingness to face danger head-on made it far too big a risk for her heart. She'd loved and lost once before, and she had no desire to do it again.

Mia stirred, and Gabby picked her up again and started singing to her. She needed confirmation that Mia was safe. Needed to feel her baby sleeping against her chest. Needed to breathe in the familiar scent of baby lotion and powder while trying not to think about how close she'd come to losing her little girl. And how that reality still terrified her.

And Liam... No matter what her heart said, she couldn't lose him, either.

God, I've pushed You away for so long. Coming back to You only when I need something seems wrong, but I need You. Not just today, but every day. And I need Liam to be okay.

She stood at the window with Mia until she knew she couldn't stay awake any longer. Marci had promised her again to update her if anything happened. In the meantime, she'd just have to trust, and try—as hard as it was—to let go of the fear and panic. Because for now there was nothing she could do. She'd just have to trust that God would protect him and bring him home safely tomorrow.

She laid Mia down on the bed next to the giraffe that Gus had washed and dried—almost as good as new. She only wished she knew how long it would be until *she* felt as good as new. Letting out a deep sigh, she closed her eyes and prayed for sleep.

FOURTEEN

The frigid wind swept through Liam as he weighed his options. While he was grateful Maldin hadn't shot him, a bullet wasn't the only threat he'd faced today. He was already shivering, and it wasn't going to be long until the beginning stages of hypothermia started to set in.

Memories of his time in the field while on active duty surfaced—ruck marches, rehydrated meals and long nights of training in remote locations. But tonight he couldn't let the cold flowing through his body gain any ground. He picked up his pace down the narrow, tree-lined road and started working on a plan. It wasn't likely that he'd run into another car out here in the middle of nowhere, which meant that for now, he was on his own. Darkness had already settled in around him, dropping the temperatures further, but at least the sky had cleared and it wasn't snowing any more.

He jogged in the direction of the main road, mentally going through his limited options. He could hunker down, build a basic emergency shelter, and try to get a fire going for warmth while waiting for someone to find him, but there was only one obvious solution in his mind. He felt for the receiver he'd dropped into his pocket after finding it on Thatcher's body. His plan was simple. He'd managed to plant the tracking device they'd found on Gabby in Maldin's jacket during the man's escape to the car. Combined with the receiver, the authorities should be able locate Maldin. But in order to stop him, Liam needed help deactivating the jammer he was certain Maldin was still using, and he had to get the receiver to someone who could read it before the man got into the air. Which meant he was running out of time.

Headlights appeared on the horizon, temporarily shifting Liam's attention. He picked up his pace, lifting up a prayer at the same time, that whoever was behind the wheel would help him. A minute later, he stepped out into the middle of the road and waved down the vehicle until it came to a stop.

"Sir—" the driver stepped out of the car

"—it's a pretty cold night to be out here. Are you okay?"

Liam let out a long sigh of relief. "I am now. I'm Captain Liam O'Callaghan, and I need your help."

At three forty-five in the morning, Liam stood in the doorway of the room where Gabby slept, hesitant to wake her. His mother had insisted she wanted him to let her know he was okay, but he also knew she needed her sleep. The past few days had taken a toll on them, both mentally and physically. Watching her sleep reminded him of how grateful he was that she was alive and safe. Things could have ended so differently.

The soft glow from an outside security light shone through the window and across Gabby's face. Mia lay on the bed next to her, her curls splayed across her cheek. He knocked softly on the open door, then crossed the hardwood floor and sat down on the edge of the bed.

"Gabby?" He gently shook her shoulder.

"Liam…" She sat up, eyes wide open as she looked at him. "You're here. What happened?"

"My mom said you wanted me to wake you up. And honestly… I couldn't wait until morning to see you and make sure you're really okay."

"We're fine. Both of us." She touched his cheek briefly, then pulled away. "But you... You're the one I've been worried about. What happened? How did you get away from him?"

"I'll tell you about everything in the morning, because honestly it's been a long night." The little sleep he'd gotten over the last couple nights was beginning to affect him. "But Maldin had me drive him to an airstrip where he'd managed to get a ride from a pilot friend of his. He left me to walk twenty miles back to the main road, thinking he'd be long gone by the time I found help."

"It's freezing out there, dark and you didn't even have your coat—"

"I know, but a local astronomy group was headed out to the airstrip to do some stargazing. Told me they were there because it's the best time of year. Something about when the temperature drops and the humidity in the air turns to ice crystals, you end up with a more transparent sky and better views. But I told them it was no coincidence."

She shook her head. "I never stopped praying. And I'm not the only one."

"I know."

"What time is it?"

"Just before four." He glanced toward the

windows. "Sun's going to be up in a couple of hours—"

"And you need sleep."

"Agreed." He studied her face in the soft light, wishing she didn't affect his heart the way she now did. But everything that had happened over the past couple days had proven to him it was something he couldn't ignore. It wasn't simply going to go away. "I might not see anyone again till noon. Mom's promised to fix us all a big brunch once I'm up."

"I'd like that."

Mia stirred next to Gabby.

"I don't want to wake her up."

"You're fine." Gabby picked up the giraffe that had rolled to the edge of the bed and put it back in Mia's arms. "She's still sound asleep. It's like she's already forgotten what happened. But it's going to be a long time before I forget."

"She's resilient. Just like her mama."

"What about Maldin?" Gabby asked.

"The authorities just arrested him. Which means it's all over now."

She shook her head. "How did they end up tracking him?"

"After the colonel shot Thatcher, I searched his pockets and found the receiver he'd used to track us. I was counting on the fact that Maldin would dump me somewhere, because I still had the tracker they planted on you."

"So you turned it on and planted it on him?"

"Not a bad plan if I do say so myself. Especially after they were able to deactivate his jammer."

She swung her feet over the edge of the bed and caught his gaze. "You could have told me about your plan. Given me a hint that you were going to be okay, because I was so worried." She didn't even try to fight the tears. "I was so afraid he was going to kill you. You saved my daughter and I will be forever grateful, but I didn't want to lose you. And I thought…"

He squeezed her hand. "I wanted to tell you, but there was no way."

"I know, I just…" She pressed her lips together. "I'm glad you're okay."

"We're all okay. And that's all that matters."

"You say it's over, but what about Colonel Peterson? Do we know the truth about him?"

"I asked Griffin on the way here. They've been digging into his background. According to Maldin, he never was told who they were working for. And despite what Thatcher said, there is still no evidence that Peterson was ever involved."

Her gaze shifted to the floor.

"You don't agree?" he asked.

"I still have questions. What reason did Thatcher have to make up a story like that? It doesn't make sense. He was scared. I'm just not convinced yet that he was lying. But we might never know, because he's dead."

"I agree, but even I can't deny that Peterson killed him in self-defense."

"So that's it? It's over?" she asked.

"Not yet. Griffin is convinced—as am I— that there is still someone on the inside involved."

"Like Peterson?"

"If it is Peterson, the authorities will find out the truth." He studied their entwined fingers, fighting against his heart's longing to kiss her. "Peterson also asked if he could talk to us tomorrow...well, today. Apparently, he wants to explain his side of this."

"Sounds noble of him. Making sure we don't have any unanswered questions left."

He caught the sarcasm in her voice. "I'm still not sold on his innocence, either, but at the least we need to listen to the man."

"I agree. And I'm ready to put an end to all of this, but if there's any chance—any chance at all—he's involved—"

"For now, we both need to sleep. Things will look clearer in the morning, and we'll feel better."

She nodded, then looked up at him. "Liam… thank you. You knew the risks in what you did, and yet you still went with him. You put your life on the line and saved Mia and me. I'll never be able to repay you, but thank you."

"There's no way I'd let anything happen to the two of you. But we're all safe. That's all that really matters right now."

He kissed her on the forehead, then left the room. There were other things he wanted to say to her. Questions he wanted to ask her, like was she feeling the same things he was. Because everything at this moment seemed to be filled with uncertainties. His career, his future and now somehow Gabby stepped into his life and made those issues not seem to matter as much as they used to. It was as if being with her was the final piece of the puzzle he was looking for in his life. The piece that made everything right again.

But falling for her still seemed so unexpected. And until he knew how she felt…

He stepped into his room and shut the door behind him. He sat down on the bed and pulled off his boots. He was exhausted, which meant that now wasn't the time to process how he felt. There would be time for that in the days and weeks to come. Because if she felt even a fraction of what he did, he knew he was going to have to take things slow. She'd loved and lost, and he was pretty sure her heart wasn't ready to jump into another relationship. Especially with all the risks involved in loving a soldier.

He'd find a way to let her know how he felt while at the same time ensuring her that there was no rush. Because he was willing to wait for her until she was ready to open her heart again.

"Gabby…"

Gabby looked up from her half-empty plate of eggs, bacon and biscuits the next morning to where Liam sat next to her at the kitchen table. "Sorry. My mind's a million miles away."

"I can tell," Liam said. "You've barely spoken a dozen words since we sat down."

"I'm sorry."

"Don't be. I just want to make sure you're okay."

She smiled at him, still tired despite sleeping until Mia woke her up at nine o'clock.

Mia banged on the tray of the high chair on the other side of her, sending a Cheerio into the air and landing on the floor. Gabby grabbed her daughter's chubby fist and kissed it. "We're not going to be invited back if you keep making messes."

Mia just grinned, then shoved a piece of strawberry into her mouth.

Marci topped up their coffees and laughed. "I had four boys, remember. This is nothing."

"You deserve a medal," Gabby said.

"I'd say they turned out pretty good, which is better than any medal in my book."

"Sounds like Griffin just drove up with the colonel." Liam nodded toward the front door. "You ready for this?"

"I don't know." She glanced out the window, unable to deny that Colonel Peterson was the source of her anxiety. "I just saw the man shoot someone. I don't know if I'm ever going to be able to erase that from my mind."

"I know this is hard, but I think he will be able to answer some of our questions."

She caught his gaze. "You think he'll also be able to convince us he's not involved in this?"

"That's what I'm hoping."

Griffin stepped into the kitchen alone. "Good morning. I hope the two of you were able to get some sleep."

Liam stood up from the table. "It was a short night, but at least I'm home."

"I agree. Are you both ready to talk to the colonel? He needs to head back to the base right after this."

"You both go on in there," Marci said. "I'll get Mia cleaned up."

Gabby started for the living room, then stopped. "Griffin... I'm hoping you're still planning to do a thorough investigation into what happened."

"I can assure you that our investigation is far from over."

"I know, and I'm sorry. Everything that has happened has shaken me up."

"Which is completely understandable."

"Can I ask him questions?" she asked.

"Whatever you want."

The colonel stood in the middle of the living room with his hands clasped behind his back. A fragment of guilt surfaced. What right did she have to question his loyalty to his country?

"Captain O'Callaghan... Mrs. Kensington..." The colonel took a step forward. "I appreciate you both meeting with me, though I'm sorry it has to be under these circumstances. And I'm so sorry for everything you've had to go through." He turned to Gabby. "I honestly can't imagine how terrifying it was to have your daughter taken so soon after losing your husband. I was thrilled to hear she's safe."

"Thank you. I appreciate your concern."

"Your husband was a hero and died a hero.

Don't ever forget that his service to our country was not in vain."

"I won't. Thank you."

"You have to understand that Thatcher was never stable. I tried to help him on several occasions, but he was never able to be the soldier your husband was and maybe that's why he did what he did. He was disillusioned and honestly needed help, which is why I'm not really surprised at what happened. I just wish he could have received that help, because things never should have ended the way they did."

"I agree, sir," Liam said.

"Do you have any questions for me?" the man asked.

Gabby pressed her lips together before speaking. "There are some things that are still bothering me. Thatcher told us he did the things he did because you hired him. Hired him to search my house, and ultimately to scare me into giving you evidence my husband had about your involvement with a military contractor who managed to defraud our government."

Colonel Peterson clasped his hands behind him. "That's quite an accusation, but I can understand, considering the circumstances, why you might believe the things he said."

"While I hate to imagine that's true," she

continued, "I don't understand his motivation to do something like this on his own."

"Unfortunately, we never will, but the bottom line is that there isn't any evidence, if I understand correctly."

She shook her head. "No, there isn't."

"Which seems to me that he was disillusioned about something. I'm just very sorry you and your baby ended up in the crosshairs of this situation. My only words of consolation to you are that Thatcher—and the man he was working with—are no longer a threat to either of you."

Gabby nodded. "And for that I am grateful. But I do have a couple more questions if you don't mind."

"Of course."

"Why did you seem to go along with him on the phone? If there really wasn't any money—"

"There were hostages' lives involved. You, Captain O'Callaghan... I decided I didn't want to anger him any more than he already was. And if I could find a way to buy more time, then the authorities would be able to step in and stop this. Arguing with him wasn't going to work because I knew he wouldn't listen. But the money he wanted was nothing more than an illusion. I'll be retiring on my army pension and nothing else. I can guarantee you that."

She nodded, wanting to believe his explanation, but she still wasn't fully convinced. "Do you have any idea why Kyle Thatcher did what he did?"

"I've been talking to the deputy here, trying to answer that very question. It is possible that your husband crossed paths with Thatcher at some point. There might have even been a confrontation between the two. Accusations against Thatcher about his involvement in government theft. If he heard you were asking questions about your husband's death and he was involved, Thatcher would have wanted to stop the truth from coming out."

"So he decided to ensure that didn't happen."

"That would be my explanation." He reached out and shook Liam's hand and then hers. "I need to head back to the base, and I'm sure you both need to rest. Again, I truly am sorry for your loss and all that the two of you have had to go through over the past few days. And I'm glad your daughter is safe."

"Thank you, Colonel. I appreciate it."

"I hope that having the chance to talk in a more neutral location will help all of us put this behind us."

Gabby watched them walk out the front door to the car, then sat down on the edge of the couch. The realization of how close she'd come to losing Mia settled over her afresh. Maybe everyone was right. Maybe she just needed to be grateful her daughter was safe and put it all behind her.

Liam sat down next to her. "What are you thinking?"

"I need to put all this behind me. I realize that. And while Thatcher was apparently a very good actor—or maybe very disillusioned—everything the colonel said made sense. Seemed believable. To think that Thatcher was just saying all those things in hopes of framing the colonel…" She felt a shiver slide through her despite the gas fireplace crackling in the corner of the room. She shook her head. "I want to believe him."

"But you don't?"

She shook her head.

"I know none of it seems to make sense," Liam said. "Especially after hearing Thatcher, but there's nothing we can do. Griffin and the other deputies will do a thorough investigation to make sure they didn't miss something. But honestly, I think all we can do at this point is be thankful it's over, Gabby. It's time to let things go. Time to put all of this behind us."

"Do you think Will's suspicions were

wrong?" She blinked back the tears. "He seemed so certain."

"I don't know. We might never know, and as hard as that is, we're going to have to find a way to live with it."

"What if I can't?" The familiar doubts had begun to resurface. "When the colonel walked away from Thatcher's body, it was as if he were relieved because he'd silenced the man. And the way he looked at me… It wasn't like a man filled with regret. Instead, it was like all the loose ends had finally come together."

"Thatcher was the only witness who has said that the colonel was behind this. If there is no evidence, no proof of what he did, there's nothing more that can be done."

She looked up and caught his gaze. "But we're witnesses, aren't we? Thatcher told us what happened. Why would he have made all that up. It doesn't make sense. Nothing makes sense about the whole situation. And remember, this nightmare started after I found Will's letters and started calling around asking questions, and the colonel was one of the men I spoke with."

"But without any evidence to the contrary, I just don't know what else we can do."

"Sorry to interrupt." Marci carried a squirming Mia into the living room. "I think someone wants her mama."

Gabby took Mia into her arms and kissed her on the top of her head.

Oh, sweet baby, I came so close to losing you.

The thought surrounded her like a crushing weight and brought with it a cache of unwanted memories. The knock on her door when Will had died... The blur of his funeral... The realization she was on her own... Mia's empty crib here at the ranch...

Liam took her hand, as if he sensed what she was feeling. She felt the rush of adrenaline at his touch and knew she was losing her heart to him.

But that was something she couldn't afford. Her heart couldn't handle losing anyone else she loved, because even if she wanted to explore what was happening between them, he'd leave her for deployment and one day...one day he wouldn't come back.

FIFTEEN

Gabby sank onto the couch in the small sitting area outside the guest room and let out a soft sigh. As tired as she'd been, Mia had finally managed to go down for her nap. Hopefully, she'd sleep long enough that she wouldn't be grouchy the rest of the day. Otherwise, Gabby would probably be in for a long night.

She closed her eyes, relishing the momentary quiet surrounding her. She'd hoped to find time to get caught up with some of her work this afternoon, but between her fatigue and her inability to focus, she'd instead decided she needed to send out a letter to her clients affected. She wouldn't give specifics; just tell them the temporary delay was due to a personal emergency in her family.

No one would believe the truth.

"Gabby?" Liam came up the stairs and stopped in front of her. "Hey… Mom wanted me to ask you what your favorite pie is."

"My favorite pie?" Gabby let out a low laugh. "You do realize if I stay here much longer, I'm going to end up gaining at least five pounds. Maybe more."

He sat down in the chair across from her. "While enjoying every minute of it, I hope."

"Oh, I'll admit she's a far better cook than I am, and yes, I'm enjoying her food. Way too much."

"What's your answer?"

She shot him a smile. "Cherry, but she doesn't have to make a pie. Seriously."

"Is Mia asleep?"

"I had my doubts for a while if she would ever fall asleep, but yes, though she'll probably be up again soon. At least I was able to get a little work done. Actually, I was able to postpone work for another day or two."

"Good." He glanced to where Mia was sleeping. "How is she?"

"More resilient than I am." Gabby pulled her legs up under her. "She still seems a bit clingy, but really, you'd never know she'd been through anything. All she wanted to do was play before she finally crashed."

"And you? How are you feeling?"

"Like I'm coming out of some dark tunnel. I still can't shake the fact that I almost lost her, Liam."

"I want you to know that what you're feeling is a hundred percent normal." He leaned toward her and rested his elbows against his thighs. "Someone took your daughter from you. It's okay to be mad, sad and even to grieve. Because you've not only had to deal with Mia's kidnapping, you've been forced to relive Will's death. And that in itself is an emotional rollercoaster I'm sure you would have preferred to avoid."

She caught his gaze, surprised not for the first time how his presence managed to act like a balm on her heart. "Sounds like you know a thing or two about loss."

"I'd say we both do."

She bit the edge of her lip, suddenly feeling self-conscious. "Thank you."

"For what?"

"For returning my call. For coming to my rescue. For being there when I thought my world was about to end. I can't stop thinking about what could have happened. You risked your life for Mia and me, and I... I was so afraid I was going to lose you."

"But you didn't."

"I know."

He moved next to her on the couch and pulled her into his arms. She felt herself relaxing as she laid her head against his shoul-

der. His arms around her felt strong. Steady...
safe... And yet, this wasn't a place she could
lose herself. She would be leaving soon, and
she had no intention of leaving a piece of her
heart behind. Loving and losing again wasn't
a place she intended to go.

She pulled back from his embrace, wishing
he didn't have that mesmerizing effect on her.
"I have something I need to ask of you, but it's
a pretty big favor."

"Anything."

"I know I'm probably the only one, but I
can't get rid of the nagging feeling that Colonel Peterson was involved in all of this."

"To be honest, I can't shake that feeling, either. Do you have an idea?"

"Maybe. Will's footlocker is back at my
town house, and I'd like to go through it one
last time. I wondered if you'd help me. I need
to let this go, but I also need to make sure—
one final time—that I didn't miss anything."

"Going through Will's things can't be easy
for you, and on top of that, you're going to have
to deal with your house that was trashed. Are
you sure you want to do this so soon? You've
been through so much the past few days, and
this only brings with it more reminders—"

"It took me about a year before I could even
open it. I'd say that was progress. But yeah...

I know I need to let it go, but I just… I guess I'm still looking for my own answers. Even if it's just figuring out what Thatcher's motivation was."

"With him dead, I'm not sure we can, Gabby."

"I know. But it still doesn't make sense. We can't even prove that he knew Will. But then why target me? None of this seemed random. I know it's a long drive, and I'm asking a lot—"

"I don't mind at all." He smiled at her. "And besides, the pie will be here waiting for us when we get back."

It was half past five by the time they made it to her town house. She pulled out the chest, then started laying out all of Will's things on the coffee table in her living room, trying to ignore the rest of the house. She'd have to deal with the mess later. For now, she simply had to find a way to put all of this to rest once and for all.

Everything was there—his uniforms, the letters she'd written him. His camera with photos he'd taken… She sat cross-legged on the floor and started searching through it all methodically, looking for that one clue she was still convinced he'd left. She stopped at a photo of Will and Liam wearing fatigues and grinning at the camera and showed it to Liam.

"We ended up playing an impromptu game

of football that day. It was a nice change from the grueling sweeps and field assignments."

"You were always a good friend to him. He loved you like a brother."

"The feeling was mutual."

She set down the photo and started through another pile of letters. Liam was right. It was time for her to let go of all this. There was nothing here and nothing was going to change or give her the answer she wanted. Nothing would help prove that Thatcher had been telling the truth.

"You okay?"

She dropped the letter onto the pile, then sat back against the couch. "It's hard. Like saying goodbye again. And I suppose I'm wishing now I'd brought Mia with me. I know she's fine, but I can't stop worrying."

"She is fine. And as much as I wanted to find something, too, I just don't think the evidence is here. Or at least anything that's connected to the colonel."

"So, Thatcher did all of this on his own to find whatever evidence Will might have and save himself. When things went bad, he tried to blame it on the colonel."

"That's what it looks like to me."

"Okay." She stood up and stretched her back that had knotted up. "Then I think it's time to stop. Whatever I'm wanting to find just isn't here. The colonel was right after all. There isn't any evidence, which means for all of the unanswered questions... I guess we'll never know."

"I did have one other thought." Liam set the field notebook he'd been reading through back into the trunk. "What about his phone or his email account? Did you talk to people he might have contacted before he died? Someone he might have told about his suspicions."

"I read through his email account and looked through his phone after they gave it to me," she said, following his lead and starting to put things away. "The only people he really spoke to were me, his parents and a few friends. There was nothing in there that stood out to me."

"Clearly, he was careful."

"Maybe he was too careful."

"Did he have any other email accounts?" Liam asked.

"Another account. You know... I can't believe I never thought of that, because he did." She grabbed her computer out of her bag, surprised she hadn't remembered, but certain it would simply be another dead end. "It was one he didn't use often. He told me at one point he had no idea why he even kept it because it was only full of junk mail."

"I confess, I have one of those."

She opened the computer and went to the online website. "He used my laptop some when he was home, so I shouldn't need a password."

His account popped up, along with a long list of unopened messages in his in-box. She shoved aside the painful reminder. There was one email in the draft box.

She opened up the drafts, then clicked on the email and started reading it.

"Anything important?" Liam asked.

Her heart pounded. "Liam… I think I just found what we're looking for."

Liam sat down next to her on the couch. "What is it?"

"An email with photos and documents attached." She started opening the attachments. "Liam, this has to be it. It's dated the day before he was killed. He was getting ready to send all of it to me."

"What does his letter say?" Liam asked.

"You need to read it yourself."

He took the computer from her and started reading through the email that brought with it the stark reminder that Will was gone.

Gabby, I can't believe I'm even writing this email. I'll leave it in the draft box for now. You're the only one who knows about this email account, so I'm praying you will check it if anything happens to me. I plan to talk to Liam, but I'm worried. Until I can ensure I've gotten proof of everyone involved, I don't want to put anyone's life at risk. I've been as subtle as I can digging for information, but I think they know.

I'm attaching all the evidence I have gathered so far, which includes a paper trail connecting Peterson to Graham. Honestly, I'm still numb from what I've discovered. I never would have imagined Colonel Peterson could be involved in something like this. He might have lost three wives to the army, but his biggest mistake was going into business with Daniel Graham. Finding hard evidence has been almost impossible—the man knows how to hide his tracks—but I've attached files that should be enough evidence to prove his involvement.

If something does happen to me before I turn this in, go to Liam and show him what I have. He'll know who to go to. I know I mentioned at least once that James Casada might have answers, but I haven't been able to get ahold of him yet.

Gabby...never forget how much I love you and the baby. There's nothing more I want than for us to be together as a family. But if that doesn't happen, I want you to move for-

ward with your life and find the happiness
again that I found with you.

"Gabby..." The lights in the house flickered.
He glanced at the ceiling lamp, hoping the bad
weather wouldn't affect the power in the area.
"I know how personal this is..."

"I'll be okay." She pressed her lips together
as if trying at the same time to hold herself together. "I just wish I'd found this sooner. Wish
Will would have gone to someone he could
have trusted and turned this over to them."

"According to the date on this email, he
didn't have a chance. He died later that day."

Her eyes glistened with tears. "Do you think
the colonel was behind the IED that killed
him?"

"We might never find out, but it seems like
too much of a coincidence to dismiss it."

She nodded. "I agree."

"You were right all along. Thatcher was telling the truth. Colonel Peterson was behind all
of this."

"And he almost got away with it."

Nausea swept through him, knowing how
close they had come to letting the man get away
with murder. He started going through the documents Liam had left behind, the picture of
what had happened suddenly becoming clear.

"It looks like after all these months Peterson believed he had gotten away with everything. Will, the one person who had questioned what was going on, was dead, and the money from Graham was safe in an offshore account."

Gabby glanced at Liam. "But then I started asking questions."

"Which scared him. According to what I'm seeing so far, Peterson is only three months from retirement, which has to be why he panicked when he received your call. He knew if he was going to get away with it, he needed to make sure you didn't have any evidence of his involvement."

"He tried to squelch any concerns I had on the phone, but when he found out I'd spoken to another one of Will's commanding officers, he knew it wasn't going to be enough."

"So he decided to hire Kyle Thatcher to make sure you didn't ask any more questions."

"Thatcher probably wasn't the best choice. An old recruit of his whose moral compass wasn't far off from Peterson's. He might not have planned to kill Casada, but when he did, he panicked."

A shiver ran through her. Everything was finally coming together.

"Peterson first has him scare you by bugging your phone and threatening you," Liam said. "Next he has Thatcher search your house for evidence. When he doesn't find anything, Peterson tells him to keep following you in order to find out what you have."

Gabby nodded. "With my phone bugged, he would have known I was going to see Casada. They had to find out what Casada might know before we got there, but when Casada found them searching his home, shots were fired—"

"It changed the game," Liam said.

"Thatcher realized they were in trouble and, on top of that, he decided he wasn't going to prison for the colonel. He knew—or dug around and found out—that the colonel had money stashed away. A lot of it. And he decided that was going to be his ticket out. Taking Mia was meant to get back at the colonel for money. He was going to frame Peterson and the whole scheme would blow up in the colonel's face."

"I need to call my brother." Liam grabbed his phone from the edge of the coffee table, then stopped on hearing a creak on the kitchen floor.

Someone else was in the house.

SIXTEEN

Gabby froze as Liam shoved her phone into her hand. This was no coincidence. No burglar. She heard the familiar creak of the flooring in the kitchen and tried to fight off the wave of panic. Someone had broken into the house. And she knew exactly who it was.

"Call 911." Liam's voice was barely above a whisper. "But first get out of the house through the front door. Go to a neighbor's."

"Liam—"

"Go. Now." The lights flickered again. "I'll be right behind you."

She stumbled to her feet, feeling numb. They'd just found Will's evidence proving that the colonel had been behind this, and immediately someone had broken into her house. That had to mean someone was watching her. Listening. But how?

She unlocked the front door, trying to ignore the flood of questions. Had Peterson somehow bugged her house? Heard what they'd found and now planned to stop them in order to save himself?

"Step away from the door."

Gabby froze, then turned around slowly at the booming voice. Peterson stood at the edge of the living room, no longer a decorated soldier but a man who'd sold out his country. A man who was willing to do anything—including murder—to save his own skin. How had that happened to him? What had made him cross the line? She focused on the gun he held pointed at her. The answer to those questions didn't matter at the moment. All she knew was that she'd seen him murder a man in cold blood, and she knew he wouldn't hesitate to do it again.

"What do you want?" Liam asked.

"For you to shut up." He held out his hand toward her. "Give me the phone, slowly. Then sit down on the couch. Both of you."

She handed it to him before moving to sit down next to Liam. "You bugged my house."

"Obviously a good decision looking back." He set her phone down on the coffee table, then grabbed the laptop. "Just what I was hoping. The email hasn't been sent. He wouldn't give up, your husband. Always poking into things that weren't his business. Asking too many questions. Like the two of you."

Gabby's heart pounded. "Did you kill him?"

"Does it matter?"

"It does."

"Not directly. It was more like David and Bathsheba. You remember that story, don't you? In order for David to cover his sins, the king sent Uriah out in front where the fighting was the fiercest. The rest was inevitable."

"You meant for our entire unit to die that day," Liam said.

"One of the consequences of war."

"You won't get away with any of this," Liam said. "Because if I remember correctly, David paid for his sins in the end. And so will you. We know the truth now."

"That's where you're wrong, though I am going to have to ensure you don't tell anyone."

Gabby felt a shiver run up her spine. "You're going to kill us."

"Unfortunately for you, I don't have another option. I'm just trying to figure out the least messy way."

She glanced around the living room, desperate for a way out. At least she'd decided at the last minute not to bring Mia with her. But leaving her baby to grow up an orphan... No.

That wasn't an option, either. There had to be a way to stop this man once and for all.

"You're fooling yourself if you really think you can get away with this," Liam said. "My brother knows where we are, and how long do you think it will take them before they put two and two together and realize what's going on?"

"Long enough for me to clean all this up." He pushed Delete, then slammed the computer shut. "I've been careful to make sure nothing can come back to me. If it wasn't for that email, you never would have been able to tie me to any of this. And if there happens to be an unfortunate accident tonight—"

"An accident?" she asked.

"The weather's pretty bad out there. Do you know how easy it is for a car to spin out of control and run off the road? An accident like that could snuff out the lives of whoever was in the car in an instant."

The power flickered again, then went off and darkness flooded the house. Gabby heard a scuffle then a shot rang out, shattering the lamp beside her.

"Gabby, get out of here!"

She dove behind the couch, then heard a sharp crack followed by a groan as the men fought in the darkness on the other side of the room. Liam might be in good shape, but Peterson had at least thirty pounds on him. And in the dark… No. No matter what Liam said, she couldn't leave him. She needed to find the phone. Needed to find a way to give Liam the advantage.

She felt for the coffee table, ran her fingers across the top of it, then grabbed the phone. A second later, she swiped the screen for the flashlight and turned it on. Peterson was swinging his fist at Liam.

"Liam, watch out!"

Liam ducked at the sound of Gabby's command, barely missing being struck by Peterson's right hook. The unexpected cover of darkness had given him a moment's advantage, allowing him to lunge at the man, but now, with the light from the phone, he could engage in a more targeted attack. He dove at Peterson like a linebacker for a second time, hoping to make up for the older man's bulk by being quicker.

Peterson stumbled backward at the assault, unable to keep his footing as Liam tackled him to the ground, knocking the gun out of his hand in the process. The older man tried to grab for the weapon, but Liam was quicker and managed to pin down the man's arm.

Peterson swung at him with his free hand,

clipping Liam's cheekbone, then tried to come at him again.

"Don't move." Gabby stood over them with Peterson's gun pointed at the man. "Because like you, I will shoot if I have to."

The lights flickered back on as Peterson tried to get up, but Liam shoved his boot onto the man's shoulder. "I wouldn't move if I were you. From what I hear, she's a pretty good shot."

"He came prepared with zip ties." Gabby nodded at the floor.

As Gabby held the gun, Liam grabbed the zip ties that had fallen out of the man's pocket. He quickly tied the man's hands behind him, then moved to secure his feet, irritated at Gabby for not running, but grateful for her help. Except for the shiner he was probably going to have, thankfully neither of them had been badly hurt in the ordeal.

Her hands shook as she handed him the gun she'd been holding.

"Call 911 and get us some help. I'm going to call my brother."

She nodded.

"Griffin…" Liam said as soon as his brother picked up, his attention still on Peterson. "We found Will's evidence. Colonel Peterson lied about everything."

"Where are you?"

"At Gabby's townhouse. We came to look through Will's locker when Peterson showed up—"

"What? Are you okay?"

"I've got a shiner and probably a couple bruised ribs, but you should see the other guy." Liam let out a low laugh, feeling the need to break the tension hanging in the air. "But seriously, we're both okay."

"Are the local police there?"

"On their way. Gabby just called 911, and as for Peterson, well…" Liam glanced at the former soldier as sirens whined in the distance. "He's certainly not going anywhere."

Twenty minutes later, Liam was answering the police's questions, something that was beginning to feel oddly routine. Which was fine by him—as long as this was the last time.

Gabby was sitting on the edge of the couch, shoulders slumped and hands folded in her lap, when he finished giving his statement to the officer. All he could think about was getting her out of here and away from all of this. Because what she'd gone through the past forty-eight hours would have crushed even the strongest person.

She looked up at him, her eyes dark. "They wouldn't let me clean up the house. Said it was a crime scene now and CSI still had to finish processing everything."

"I know, but we don't have to stay." He stepped up next to her. "The detective in charge just gave us the go ahead to leave. They will make sure everything is secure when they are finished."

"I need to get back to Mia. I'm glad she wasn't with us, but this mess…"

"You can deal with this in a couple days. And you won't have to do it alone."

Things could be replaced. Their lives couldn't.

"Thank you." She grabbed her phone and stood up. "I'm ready."

"Are you sure you're okay?" he asked.

"Just feeling very shaken."

He studied her face as they walked out the front door. "By the way…you are a good shot, aren't you?"

She shook her head. "I'm a terrible shot, actually."

"Really?" He let out a low chuckle. "I'm glad I didn't know that earlier. But thank you. You saved my life. Picking up both the phone and gun was fast thinking, and on top of that, I managed to miss that first right hook."

"You'll have a bruise from the second." She

took his hand. "But I'd say it was the other way around, actually. You saved my life."

"We'll call it even then. What I do know for sure is that I think we can finally put all this behind us."

What he wasn't sure about was how he was going to put his feelings for her behind him.

SEVENTEEN

Two days later, Gabby had just finished putting the dishes into the dishwasher when a car pulled up in front of the house.

"I appreciate your help." Marci stepped into the kitchen with three more glasses. "Griffin's here. Liam told me he wanted to give you both an update in person."

Marci set the glasses on the top rack, then turned to Gabby. "Remember that the truth often works like a salve. It helps heal. And on top of that, more often than not, God manages to redeem situations that seem unredeemable. That's what I'm praying for in this situation."

"Thank you."

Mia threw one of her toys and started fussing from where she was sitting in her high chair.

Marci shook her head. "Don't worry about Mia. I think you have to have realized by now how much I'm enjoying her. Griffin is going to want to talk to you."

Gabby thanked Marci, then kissed Mia on the forehead before heading to the living room. The waiting had been the hardest part. They'd been able to recover Will's email, but after handing over all the evidence, there was nothing else they could do but wait. That, and pray those involved would soon be behind bars.

Liam walked into the room right behind her. "You have good news, we hope?"

Griffin took off his coat, then sat down on the edge of the couch. "I have to admit that even I'm surprised how quickly all of this has gone down, but once we were able to verify Will's evidence, we put together formal charges. And we ended up taking them by surprise. Just over an hour ago, authorities in Las Vegas picked up Daniel Graham and arrested him for his collaboration with the colonel in this mess. Apparently, he'd come back into the country for his daughter's wedding and she posted photos on Facebook and even tagged her father. Not a very smart move.

"The investigation isn't finished, but I'm pretty confident that they will both be going away for a very long time. Which means you're safe. Both of you."

Gabby let out a soft sigh of relief. "Thank

you. For everything. All of you. I just never imagined that my desire to find out the truth would affect so many people."

"You did everything right. Though there is one other thing." Griffin caught her gaze and she felt the worry niggling through her again. "I know this must feel like you're having to re-live everything all over again, and for that I am very sorry. But you need to know something else. Because of the information you gave us, the army will be further investigating Will's death to see if Colonel Peterson needs to be charged with your husband's murder."

She pressed her fingers against her mouth and tried to fight down the wave of nausea. She might have already suspected what he was telling her, but hearing Griffin say it out loud made it all too real.

"I want you to know," Griffin said, "as trite as it might sound at this point, your country acknowledges and truly appreciates the sacrifice you, as well as Will, made."

Gabby nodded. "Thank you. I appreciate it."

Griffin stood. "I need to head back to the station, but I felt as if I needed to tell both of you in person. There are still a lot of loose ends that need to be tied up, but that's where we are for now."

Liam walked his brother to the front door. "I know you'll keep us updated."

"I will." Griffin grabbed his coat. "Tell Mom I'll try to make it for dinner tomorrow night."

Gabby stayed on the couch, still trying to process everything Griffin had told them. Part of her felt relieved that the truth was finally out. But the other part of her still felt numb. She wasn't sure if she wanted to go bury herself away in her room or scream. How was one supposed to react to what had happened over the past few days? Maybe there was no script for the right way to feel in a situation like this.

Liam sat back down next to her. "Do you want to talk?"

"Honestly, I don't know what I need right now."

"How about a walk? The sunset's beautiful."

She nodded, feeling suddenly claustrophobic in the house. "I'd like that."

"It's not too cold, is it?"

"I'll just grab my coat and be fine. There's another layer of snow that has covered all the mountains in the background. I could never tire of the view."

He waited for her to put on her coat and beanie, then opened the front door for her. Outside the wind had died down, making the cold more bearable, but it was the view that almost made her forget the chill.

"I just wanted to make sure you were okay," Liam started, walking beside her down the gravel road. "I know all of this has to be a lot to take in. And even with all the pieces coming together, it has to be hard on you."

She nodded, wishing she could untangle her feelings toward him. But she'd save that for another day. "To be honest, my head is still reeling a bit. I feel like I came so close to losing everything that was important to me. On top of that, knowing they're going to reopen the investigation into Will's death feels like having a scab ripped off. It's like I'm having to relive everything that happened. But your mom said something earlier that stuck. God is somehow managing to bring closure for me and redeeming a situation I never thought possible. As crazy as it seems, I truly believe that this is going to go a long way toward my healing."

"I'm glad to hear that. You're a strong woman, Gabby. But no matter how strong you are, you still need give yourself time to grieve through all of this."

"I know you're right. But I also want you to know that I appreciate everything you've done for Mia and me. You went way, way beyond the call of duty, risked your life for us."

She stopped and looked up at him. "Somehow thanking you really doesn't seem adequate."

"There is one other thing I wanted to tell you."

"What's that?"

"In the middle of all of this I just heard from my commander. The doctor has cleared me, and they're finally putting me back on active duty."

"That's great news." She smiled, truly happy for him. "When do you leave?"

"There's still paperwork that has to be finished up, but I'm supposed to report for duty at Fort Carson in Colorado Springs in two weeks."

"That's wonderful. You'll be close to your family."

He glanced down at the ground, suddenly avoiding her gaze. "I'd like you to stay awhile longer if you'd want to. It would be good for you. Allow you to rest. My mother would love to spend more time with Mia and I... I'd love to spend more time with both of you before I have to report back."

She felt her breath catch at his words, realizing he wasn't asking her to stay as a friend. Things had changed between them, but she still didn't know how to interpret her own heart. If she said yes, she had a feeling that things would never be the same between them again. That there would be no going back. But her heart wasn't ready. Not now, maybe not ever. And it wouldn't be fair to him to give him hope when she knew that risking her heart loving another solider wasn't a place she wanted to go. And neither would she ever do anything to stand between the job she knew he loved and his service to his country.

"You know I'd love to stay…"

"Why do I feel as if there is a big *but* coming?"

"When your mother found out that Saturday is Mia's birthday, she insisted we stay till then. She's so excited about it, and to be honest… so am I. But after that, I'm leaving. I need to start over somewhere fresh. Make new friends and put this part of my life behind me. I've been talking with my parents. There's an open apartment in their complex in Florida. They're considering staying year-round but want to be closer to Mia. And it will be good for her to grow up close to them as well."

"What about your heart? What does it say, Gabby? I don't think I'm the only one who's felt something happen between us. I just… I don't want you and Mia to go without knowing if there's something there."

She turned away, avoiding his gaze. The

sunset had bathed the valley in stunning pink and gold. But she wasn't ready to listen to her heart. Because while it might be begging her to stay, she knew that she couldn't. Liam was the part of her life she needed closure from. To stay here—to see what might continue to develop between them—how was that going to let her put her past behind her?

"I'm sorry." She pushed away the battling thoughts and shook her head. "I don't think I can."

"Just consider it. You say you need to start over…" He took her hand and laced their fingers together. "What if you started over with me?"

Liam caught the confusion in Gabby's eyes and immediately regretted his words. He hadn't planned to say what had just come out of his mouth. At least not today. He'd pushed her too far, too soon. And on top of that, this was the day they were reopening the investigation on Will's murder. But for some reason, he couldn't stop his heart from fighting to be heard. He'd never know how she felt if he didn't try. And he wasn't ready to walk away. His brother Reid had lost his fiancée because he hadn't fought for her. Liam wasn't going to let the same thing happen with Gabby.

"I'm sorry." He caught her gaze, praying he hadn't totally pushed her away. "My timing's all wrong, and honestly, I never meant for this to happen. Somehow, in the middle of all of this, I started falling in love with you, and now I don't know how to just walk away and pretend it didn't happen."

"I know, and I'm sorry. I just can't." Gabby took a step back, the confusion on her face clear. "We can't. Life is going to go back to normal soon, but you'll always be a protector. Someone who will risk everything to make things right. It's what you do as a soldier. It's what you did with Mia and me. But that's not love. And in the end, I'll always be a reminder of what happened on the day Will died. I don't know if it's possible to separate the two, but I do know that's not a reason to love someone."

He fought the urge to pull her into his arms and kiss her like he'd wanted to for the past few days. Maybe he was crazy, but he knew if she could find a way to get past the fear, she had feelings for him as well.

"In the middle of everything that happened," he said, "I realized how afraid I was of losing you and Mia. And I don't want that to happen, Gabby. I don't want to just walk away. I don't want you to walk away. I want you in my life—both of you. Not because of Will. Not because I need to fix you or save you. Because I love you."

"I just don't think I can." Her eyes filled with tears. "There is too much baggage between us."

"If you don't feel what I'm feeling, then I'll walk away and never bring this up again. But if you are feeling anything at all toward me, don't close your heart off because you're scared of letting me in. Please. It's not because I feel sorry for you or am trying to make up for what you lost. I'll give you time…wait for you…whatever you need."

"I'm sorry." She pressed the back of her hand against her mouth, tears glistening in her eyes. "We'll stay until the party's over tomorrow, but then Mia and I are leaving."

Liam watched her walk away from him and felt his heart shatter. He waited until the screen door slammed shut behind her, then headed for the barn. That wasn't the reaction he'd expected. He'd somehow convinced himself that she felt the same way he did. Clearly, he was wrong. But losing her now? How was he supposed to watch her walk out of his life?

Or had he simply lost it?

He headed toward the barn where the horses were grazing outside nearby. Once inside, he grabbed a metal pitchfork. Physical labor had always helped him figure things out. Maybe he should have tried it before he made a fool of himself. Maybe she was right, and there was too much emotional baggage between them.

What had he been thinking?

He'd never been the impulsive type. He was never quick on decisions—more methodical and precise, unless the situation called for a swift result. And his methods had always worked well for him. But now...he wasn't even sure how this had happened. He'd never seen Gabby as a romantic interest, but clearly all of that had changed. At least it had for him.

Liam turned around as his brother Reid stepped into the barn, but didn't stop working. The last thing he wanted right now was a conversation with one of his brothers. "Just finished a shift?"

"Yeah. I wanted to make sure you were okay. Plus, I promised Dad I'd come help repair some of the fencing along the west end."

"I know he'll appreciate that."

Reid leaned against the door frame. "I don't remember you ever mucking out stalls unless Dad made you. Growing up, you preferred to do just about anything else."

"I needed to blow off some steam."

"What's going on?"

Liam frowned. Dodging questions wasn't

going to work. Reid was the one brother who could always read him. "Let's just say I put my foot in my mouth and more than likely ended up ruining everything between Gabby and me."

"How did you do that?"

"I told Gabby I've fallen in love with her." He paused, waiting for a reaction. "You don't look surprised."

"I'm assuming she didn't react the way you wanted her to."

"I thought she might feel the same way, but I was wrong."

"She said that?"

Liam leaned against the shovel. "She told me she didn't think a relationship between us was a good idea."

"Give her some time. She's been through a lot. Mom told me how she looks at you."

"Like the best friend of her husband?" He spat out the words.

"Not exactly. More like a woman who's fallen hard for someone and isn't sure how to deal with it."

"Mom's biased."

"Maybe. But even if she hasn't fallen for you, she doesn't live far. The two of you need to spend time together outside everything that's just happened."

Liam leaned the pitchfork against the stall wall. "It's more complicated than that. She's leaving for Florida to be closer to her parents."

Reid hesitated at the information. "Then what's stopping you from hopping on an airplane and going to see her?"

"I just got my orders from my commander."

"Really?" Reid let out a low whistle. "They're letting you stay in?"

"Yeah. Doctor finally says I'm deployment ready. I'm heading to Fort Carson in two weeks."

"Congratulations. Does she know that?"

"Yes. But I don't know what I was thinking. Asking her to put her heart on the line for another soldier. I'm pretty sure that's the root of all of this, and if I'm honest with myself, she doesn't deserve that. I've got four more years to serve, but for the first time in my life, I'm realizing I don't want to do this by myself. And I guess I had this idea of making a family with her and thought she might feel the same."

"Did you tell her all of that?"

"Some of it."

"Like I said. Give her some time. The last few days have dredged up Will's death. Plus, she almost lost her daughter. It's a lot to deal with."

Liam pulled off his gloves and headed out

of the stall. "Maybe, but I have a feeling I'm out of time."

"There are always options. We could have Mom invite her back up here for the holidays. Mom's hard to say no to and it would give both of you more time—"

"Thanks, but I'm not going to push her on this, and I don't need Mom as a matchmaker. I told her if she didn't feel the same way I do, I'd respect that decision, and I meant it."

"Wow... I'm sorry." Reid frowned. "I know what it's like to lose someone you love."

Liam caught the hurt in his brother's eyes, even after all these years. The woman Reid had been in love with had left him, and so far, he'd never managed to find anyone he could love the way he'd loved her.

"Sorry," Liam said.

"So am I, but I have learned something. Loving and losing...they're all a part of life. Sometimes you get your heart broken, but sometimes love lasts a lifetime."

"That's pretty profound. Almost like there's someone new in your life that you haven't told us about."

"Let's just say I've been better at giving out advice than taking it myself. I always regretted the fact that I didn't fight for Claire. Because if I had to do it all over again, trust me, I would have. Love is worth the risk, even if it doesn't work out in the end." Reid let out a low laugh. "Or at least that's what I'm still trying to convince myself of."

Liam started back to the house where his mom was reading to Mia on the veranda. He heard Mia squeal and felt his heart constrict. He wasn't supposed to feel this way for a child that wasn't his own. Wasn't supposed to have fallen in love with her mother, but somehow he had. And letting Gabby walk away? Well, he had no idea how to do that.

Gabby watched from the kitchen window the next day as Liam swung Mia around in circles on the front porch while she giggled. Her little sweetheart. The one thing that had kept her going these past months. But now…now there was someone else who made her heart want to live fully again, and she didn't know how to deal with it. She'd managed to avoid being alone with Liam yesterday, which with most of his family around hadn't been difficult. But she'd sensed his presence around her no matter where he was.

And she wasn't sure she could fight it anymore.

She let out a soft sigh. She wasn't sure exactly when or how it had happened, but Liam

O'Callaghan had managed to stir the places in her heart she'd thought were dead. Her capability to trust again. To love. To imagine that there could actually be joy after loss.

Stepping outside onto the porch, her heart melted when Mia noticed her. She walked toward Liam and kissed Mia on the side of her neck, relishing in her response as her daughter lunged into her arms.

"You're going to spoil her." She glanced at Liam. "Both you and your mother."

"I have a feeling my mother would say that it never hurt a child to receive too much love."

"I'm not complaining. She's really taken to the both of you."

Mia squirmed out of her arms, then grabbed on to Gabby's fingers so she could walk.

A second later, Mia let go.

"Mia?"

She wobbled across the porch on her own.

"Liam…" Gabby grabbed his hand. "She just took her first steps."

Mia grinned from ear to ear, clearly proud of herself before grabbing on to a potted plant for balance.

Marci stepped onto the porch. "Did she just walk?"

Gabby laughed. "She did."

"Your little girl's growing up," Liam said.

Mia teetered for a moment, then tipped the plant over, scattering dirt across the porch as she plopped down on her bottom.

"Mia!"

Marci laughed. "She's fine. I'll get her inside and get her cleaned up. Why don't the two of you sit out here and enjoy the sunshine for a few minutes. Lunch won't be for another thirty minutes, and I heard the temperature's about to drop with more snow on the way."

Gabby watched as Liam's mom took Mia into the house, leaving the two of them alone. She shifted her gaze to the horizon as a wave of self-consciousness washed over her. They needed to talk and now was as good a time as any.

"Do you mind?" he asked.

She shoved her hands into her pockets and nodded. "I'd like a walk."

She had so much to say to him, and no idea how to start.

"I have to admit," Liam said. "I've never spent a lot of time around kids, but that little girl's pretty much stolen my heart."

Gabby laughed. "Mine, too. From the first day she entered this world. Though, I still can't believe she's turning one. Doesn't seem possible."

They stood beside each other in silence for

a few moments, giving Gabby time to take in the now-familiar snowcapped mountains that rose up in the distance beyond the ranch. Giving her time to wonder how she'd managed to lose her heart. But she had.

"I feel as if I owe you a huge apology," Liam said. "I realized that I overstepped my bounds when we spoke last, but honestly, Gabby, I don't regret it. I told you I would walk away if that's what you wanted, but I meant what I said. Mia's not the only one who's stolen my heart. You have."

"Liam—"

"Wait." He turned to her. "Before you start throwing out excuses at me, just hear me out one last time. And I promise it will be the last time. But as hard as I know this must be for you, I think you feel something for me as well."

She smiled, trying not to chuckle at his serious expression. He was so focused on convincing her that he didn't even realize she already agreed.

He took her hand, not giving her a chance to respond. "I meant what I said when I told you why I'd never married. It was because I'd never found the right person. And I never would have imagined it could be you. On top of that, for this past year, all I've wanted to do was run from you and the memoires you brought. But then, somehow, you made me smile again and wonder what it would be like to have a family. And while we both know being married to a soldier isn't easy, you're the one I want to come home to. You and Mia."

She looked up and caught his gaze, her heart about to burst. "Can I talk now?"

"Of course, I just… I can't let you go without a fight. And I want you to understand—"

"Liam." She laughed, then pressed her palm against his cheek. "I wasn't going to argue with you. I hardly slept last night, wrestling with my own heart. And I realized you're right."

"What?" He dropped his hands to his side.

"I've been so caught up in surviving and doing things on my own that I honestly hadn't thought about ever falling in love again. And then, when my heart started to feel once more, it terrified me, and I only pushed you away. Part of it was the idea of being a military wife again. I know the benefits, but I also know how lonely and scary it can be. And how much can be lost. Honestly, it still scares me." She shook her head. "But somehow you made me remember it's worth it if you can be with the person you love. I want to take things slowly—need to take things slowly—but I've realized that I want to be the one you come home to."

He stared at her, his jaw slack as if he were trying to take in what she'd just said.

She smiled up at him. "Isn't that what you wanted to hear?"

"Yes, but… I guess I'm just having a hard time believing I'm not dreaming."

"Maybe this will help convince you." She stepped up to him and kissed him on the lips.

A moment later, Liam wrapped his arms around her and pulled her tighter against him, deepening their kiss until she finally pulled away, breathless.

"Convinced you're not dreaming?" she asked.

His smile widened. "You might have to convince me some more, but what do we tell my family?"

She glanced back at the front door and laughed. "Oh, I have a feeling they already know."

EPILOGUE

Eight months later, Gabby stood at the edge of the reception area with the mountains rising up in front of them, set off by wispy clouds across the pink sky ablaze from the setting sun. It was the perfect evening for an outdoor June wedding. They'd kept everything simple, just like she'd wanted. A private ceremony on the ranch with their parents, his brothers and a handful of close friends. Lanterns had been strung above them, and a live string quartet played in the background while the guests mingled.

Everything had turned out perfect.

"I can't tell you how happy we both are for you." Gabby's mother gave her a hug, then took a step back and caught her daughter's gaze. "I know you've been faced with a lot of difficult things these past couple years, but to see you smiling right now means more to me than you'll ever know."

She matched her mother's smile. "I think I do know, Mom."

Her father squeezed her hand. "We're very proud of you. And extremely happy for you."

While she might never be completely the same because of loss, Liam had come into her life and managed to put back together the broken pieces of her heart.

Liam stepped up beside her and her parents. "Would you mind excusing us for a moment? I need to speak with my wife."

Her breath caught as she looked up at him in his military dress blues. "I like the sound of that... Your wife."

Liam grabbed her hand and pulled her away from the guests, before drawing her into his arms and kissing her.

"Sometimes it felt like this day would never come, but it's been perfect."

She let out a soft laugh and wrapped her arms around his neck. "It was perfect. Though I have to admit, I think Mia stole the show today."

"What did you expect? She takes after her mother."

Gabby reached up and kissed him again, feeling her heart swell at his nearness. "Flattery will get you everywhere, you know."

She'd noted the changes that had taken place

over the past eight months in both of them. Peterson's conviction had helped erase the anxiety his criminal actions had left. No longer did she have to worry about her safety or Mia's. But the greater change had been how God had gifted her with a renewed sense of lasting peace she'd never expected. She never thought she'd ever be ready to step into the shoes of a military wife again, and while she couldn't deny moments of anxiety, with it had come a chance to enjoy each day spent with Liam.

"This time last year I had no idea what direction my life would take." Liam smiled down at her. "The army was considering discharging me, and as for falling in love…well…it wasn't even in the picture. Especially with you."

"Any regrets, Mr. O'Callaghan?" she asked.

"None at all, Mrs. O'Callaghan."

He leaned down and kissed her, this time lingering longer and sending her heart racing.

"I supposed we should go back to our guests," she said.

"As long as I can have you all to myself for the next ten days, I supposed I can share you for another hour."

Gabby hesitated. "Do you think our parents will survive keeping up with Mia for that long?"

"Please don't tell me you're having second thoughts of leaving her for our honeymoon."

"I'll miss her, but not a chance."

"Good, because I can promise you that they're going to love every minute of it. And I'm going to love every moment alone with my wife."

He took her hand and started back to where their guests were eating wedding cake and dancing beneath the stars. But the only person she could see was Liam. Her heart seemed to still for a moment. The seasons of life had brought their own share of pain, but today was a reminder of love, hope and of God's gift of second chances.

* * * * *

Dear Reader,

Thank you so much for reading Liam and Gabby's story! Not only did I love writing this novel, I loved the setting where this brand-new series is going to take place. My husband's family is from Colorado, so we've spent a lot of time in that beautiful state. The idea of a family run ranch nestled beneath such impressive views is a place I'd love to spend a long, cozy winter!

While you might never have to face some of the things Liam and Gabby did, I know there will be times in your life—maybe even right now—when things seem to spiral out of control and you find yourself desperately searching for strength and courage to face another day. My prayer for you today is that you will remember that you are not alone, and especially that you will seek to find your protection in Him.

Watch for more page-turning suspense from Timber Falls and the O'Callaghan brothers!

Lisa Harris

Get 4 FREE REWARDS!

We'll send you 2 FREE Books plus 2 FREE Mystery Gifts.

Love Inspired® books feature contemporary inspirational romances with Christian characters facing the challenges of life and love.

FREE Value Over **$20**

YES! Please send me 2 FREE Love Inspired® Romance novels and my 2 FREE mystery gifts (gifts are worth about $10 retail). After receiving them, if I don't wish to receive any more books, I can return the shipping statement marked "cancel." If I don't cancel, I will receive 6 brand-new novels every month and be billed just $5.24 for the regular-print edition or $5.74 each for the larger-print edition in the U.S., or $5.74 each for the regular-print edition or $6.24 each for the larger-print edition in Canada. That's a savings of at least 13% off the cover price. It's quite a bargain! Shipping and handling is just 50¢ per book in the U.S. and 75¢ per book in Canada.* I understand that accepting the 2 free books and gifts places me under no obligation to buy anything. I can always return a shipment and cancel at any time. The free books and gifts are mine to keep no matter what I decide.

Choose one:

☐ **Love Inspired® Romance Regular-Print**
(105/305 IDN GMY4)

☐ **Love Inspired® Romance Larger-Print**
(122/322 IDN GMY4)

Name (please print)

Address   Apt. #

City   State/Province   Zip/Postal Code

Mail to the **Reader Service:**
IN U.S.A.: P.O. Box 1341, Buffalo, NY 14240-8531
IN CANADA: P.O. Box 603, Fort Erie, Ontario L2A 5X3

Want to try 2 free books from another series! Call 1-800-873-8635 or visit www.ReaderService.com.

---

*Terms and prices subject to change without notice. Prices do not include sales taxes, which will be charged (if applicable) based on your state or country of residence. Canadian residents will be charged applicable taxes. Offer not valid in Quebec. This offer is limited to one order per household. Books received may not be as shown. Not valid for current subscribers to Love Inspired Romance books. All orders subject to approval. Credit or debit balances in a customer's account(s) may be offset by any other outstanding balance owed by or to the customer. Please allow 4 to 6 weeks for delivery. Offer available while quantities last.

Your Privacy—The Reader Service is committed to protecting your privacy. Our Privacy Policy is available online at www.ReaderService.com or upon request from the Reader Service. We make a portion of our mailing list available to reputable third parties that offer products we believe may interest you. If you prefer that we not exchange your name with third parties, or if you wish to clarify or modify your communication preferences, please visit us at www.ReaderService.com/consumerschoice or write to us at Reader Service Preference Service, P.O. Box 9062, Buffalo, NY 14240-9062. Include your complete name and address.

LI19R